LOGAN

LOGAN

ALAN JOSEPH

CUTTING EDGE

ISBN-13: 978-1-957868-03-5

Published by
Cutting Edge Books
PO Box 8212
Calabasas, CA 91372
www.cuttingedgebooks.com

CHAPTER ONE

He helped the girl up the short gangway and onto the boat. She walked with that extracarefulness of someone who knows she's had too much to drink. On the deck, he spun her around and she came to him with lips open, her mouth waiting for his. His hand found her breasts under the scoop-necked satin blouse. They were small but so soft, so very soft, and suddenly she was not a girl he'd met at a bar a few hours ago but Venus, Aphrodite, Helen of Troy.

"Here, out on the deck?" he heard her murmur and he stepped back.

"Go below," he said. "The light switch for the cabin is on the right. I'll take in the gangway and be right down."

He watched her start down the companionway, her firm, young rear wriggling in the too-tight black skirt. He hurried to pull in the gangway, and he had just set it on the deck when the scream split the night, pure terror, and loud as hell. He was down the few steps into the cabin in one bound. The girl was in the doorway, her hand still on the light switch, her body shaking, her eyes riveted on the cabin floor. Logan followed her eyes.

"Jesus Christ!" he said. Eyes, protruding and huge, stared up at him with the sightless stare of death. The girl's neck was twisted horribly, with a harsh red-blue ugly line creasing her throat. She wore only a slip and one lifeless breast had spilled out one side. Logan looked at the girl by the door.

"I'm going to be sick," she said.

"Not here you're not," he growled. He grabbed her and half-lifted, half-flung her up onto the deck and saw her fall against the rail. He turned back to the staring, twisted thing on the cabin floor. He knelt down and touched the girl's head, moving it a little, holding her by the chin with his big, powerful hands. He got up and went out on the deck. The girl from the bar had finished being sick and she was edging toward the rail near the quay, looking at Logan with wide, frightened eyes.

Logan put the short gangway back in place. "Go on, get off," he told her, grimly. She scrambled up and over onto the quay, shooting him glances that were half-apology, half-fear. Logan pushed back the peaked cap on his head and watched her disappear into the night. He wasn't surprised when two sets of headlights pierced the dark, and he saw the cars turning at the top of the hill to start slowly down the narrow quay. He wasn't surprised to see they were police cruisers. Nor was he at all surprised to see them stop in front of the *Sea Urchin*. It figured. His mind was racing, thinking of the man he'd thrown off the boat the night before. He wanted to think more about that, to replay it in his mind, but the police sergeant was talking to him.

"May we come aboard, *señor*?" the sergeant was saying. Logan smiled thinly. The Panamanian police, like most cops in Latin American countries, always started off polite. They also politely ignored a bushel of legal, civil and moral rights when they got going.

Logan indicated the cabin. "In there," he said. The sergeant told two of his men to have a look. He stayed on the deck and surveyed Logan.

"May I see your papers, captain?" he smiled. "Passport, licenses, whatever you have."

Logan handed him a cluster of glassine-covered cards and papers. One of the cops called the sergeant, his voice excited, shocked. The sergeant glanced into the cabin and turned to Logan, a subtle grimness settling onto his face.

"Who is she, *señor*?" he asked, looking balefully at the tall American with the lean, hard face.

"Goldilocks. Little Bo-peep. Ophelia. You give her a name," Logan said, matching the cop's baleful stare. "You seemed to know she was there. That's more than I did."

He felt the angry rage gathering inside him, the frustrated, churning rage of a man who knows he's been trapped. He could predict the coming sequence of questions and answers, all leading to the same, inexorable ending. It added a further edge to his already reckless temper.

"You did not know she was in the cabin of your boat," the sergeant said, patiently. "You do not expect me to believe that, do you, *señor*?"

"I don't give a shit what you believe," Logan said. "I never saw her until just now. Why don't you ask whoever told you she was here about her?"

"A phone call, what you *americanos* call a *tip*," the officer said. Logan nodded, bitterness in his eyes. He had figured that much the minute he saw their headlights swing into the quay. The sergeant returned Logan's papers.

"You have a lot of papers, *Señor* Logan, a lot of licenses," he said. "But none of them tell me what you do for a living."

"We hire out, the *Urchin* and me," Logan said. "When we feel like, where we feel like and how we feel like."

"Perhaps you hire out to murder young, blonde *señoritas*?"

"No," Logan answered, his voice hard, flat. "We do that for the fun of it."

He had the satisfaction of seeing cold anger move into the sergeant's otherwise impassive face.

"You refuse to tell us anything about the girl, eh?" he said.

"I don't *know* anything about her."

"And of course you would like it if we just forgot about the *señorita* and just went on our way," the sergeant said, a resigned smile on his face.

"No, I'd like you to take her with you," Logan said. "If nobody calls for her in thirty days she's yours."

The sergeant's face turned to stone and he nodded toward the police car. "Let us go, *Señor* Logan," he said. "We shall let you try your humor on the inspector."

Logan walked to the police car and slid into the back seat. The sergeant moved in beside him while one of the policemen took the wheel. As they moved slowly away, Logan saw the other two cops take up positions at the gangway of the *Sea Urchin*. They would wait for the coroner's wagon and then impound his boat, as they were going to impound him. He stared out the window, his mind racing, bitter thoughts tumbling over each other in their haste to sort themselves out. He was alone, in this little hole in Panama, being taken in for the murder of some chickie he'd never seen in his life. But it didn't just happen. It had been carefully set up. Once again, he was seeing the man who'd come to the *Urchin* the night before. *There* was the connection. He laughed grimly, inwardly. Some connection. He could just see the sergeant's face if he tried to tell him about the man last night. But the bastard had been real enough. Tall, thin, well-dressed, speaking English with just the trace of a South American accent. Logan replayed it in his mind, seeking something that would help him in his present spot.

The man had said he wanted to hire him and the *Urchin*. It was for a task of some delicacy and he'd promised a big chunk of loot, ten thousand dollars worth of chunk. Logan recalled how his temper had started to rise.

"All that for something delicate?" he had frowned. "You mean dangerous, not delicate. The answer is the same, anyway. No, I'm not interested."

"The people I represent will not take no for an answer," the man had said. He was an errand boy, for all his silk suit and smooth manners, Logan realized. And he was talking down to him. Nobody should talk down to anybody, ever, Logan felt. It was one of his mottos, along with enjoy.

"This'll be a new experience for them," Logan said. "Now get the hell off my boat."

"We have ways of persuading you, my friend," the man had said, putting menace into his voice. Logan put shoulder into his blow. It caught the man flush on the jaw and he went flying into the *Urchin's* rail, bounced off and rolled across the deck. He started to get up, his hand gropingly trying to reach into his inside jacket pocket. Logan clipped him again and he flipped over to hit the deck with a resounding thud. Logan picked him up as though he were a child, lifted him across the gangway and flung him onto the quay, watching his body roll across the stones to hit up against the building wall on the other side.

"How's that for persuasion, pal?" Logan had tossed after him. He recalled how he'd taken in the gangway and gone down to the cabin, fixed a good shot of Tennessee sippin' whiskey and stretched out on the bunk. He'd had the same trouble many times. People and money. He didn't go for either, except on his terms.

His thoughts snapped off as the police car rolled to a halt. There was a why to all this. He'd be finding out, he was certain. But he wasn't so sure he'd like it when be did.

CHAPTER TWO

The inspector had been called from a party, not a very good party but nonetheless a party, and he didn't like the interruption. He disliked the vermin he normally had to deal with but this one, at least, was different. Murder itself lifted this one out of the ordinary. He was meaner, too. The sergeant's briefing had told him that. Logan returned the inspector's stare under a fluorescent fight tube in the ceiling that brought a glaring brightness to the lone chair on which he sat, the small table, the dingy gray of the walls. It heightened all the contrasts, making Logan's dark eyes darker, the inspector's white suit whiter. The room, what he presumed to be the interrogation room of the jail, was thoroughly inhibiting. Logan didn't consider himself an authority on much of anything, except perhaps women and boats, certainly not jails. But this one, he guessed, would set some sort of record for unrelieved drabness. The inspector wore an air of weariness which, Logan interpreted, cloaked active hostility. Behind the inspector, in a comer of the room, stood a gray-shirted jailer who oozed evil from every pore of his body but mostly from his eyes. Logan had seen eyes like those before, always on men who enjoyed other people's pain. He saw the man's tongue move across thick lips as the jailer's eyes flicked up and down his lean, hard-packed frame. The bastard was already estimating how much pain this new one could stand, Logan knew, and once again he could predict the script. Yet it had to be played out. It had been written, the characters cast into it, all by someone else, someone who knew that each of them would play their roles, the inspector, the jailer and himself. Last night he had thrown a man off the *Urchin* and now he was paying for it.

The inspector had read the sergeant's report, conferred with his man, looked at Logan's papers and was now fastening the tall American with a world-weary eye.

"The truth, *Señor* Logan," he said. "It would save everyone a lot of time and trouble."

"It would," Logan agreed, his face expressionless. "I never saw the girl before she was dumped on my boat. That's the truth, all of it." He got up. "Feel free to call me if you find out who she was," he said. "It was nice meeting you."

He started for the door. The gray-shirted jailer was across the room instantly, blocking his way to the door, a puzzled, uncertain frown on his face.

"All right, Soyez," Logan heard the inspector say, "sit down, captain."

Logan shrugged, cast Soyez a wide grin, watching the man's frown deepen, and then turned away and sat down again.

"You have a quixotic sense of humor, I see, *amigo*," the inspector commented. "A luxury, I would say, for a man in your position."

"Everybody needs a few luxuries," Logan said, and his eyes grew cold. "You wanted the truth and you got it. So bug off and let me get the hell out of here."

"You must think we are exceptionally gullible," the inspector said, his eyes half-closed.

"No, exceptionally stupid," Logan shot back and saw the inspector's eyes narrow still further. "If that excuse for a cop had examined the body he'd have noticed that rigor mortis had already set in. She was killed at least six hours before your boys arrived."

"A mere detail," the inspector countered. "What is to say you did not kill her six hours before?"

"And leave her lying around the cabin?" Logan snorted. "That could draw flies."

The inspector's eyes widened enough for Logan to see them grow hard.

"I do not know if you killed her," the inspector said. "But she was found on your boat. This means either you or someone you know did kill her aboard your boat. In either case, you are not telling us the truth. The sergeant and I are of one mind on that."

"One mind," Logan echoed. "And each of you got half of it."

The man's eyes registered no change. Only his voice grew deadlier.

"I shall let you meditate overnight on this," he said. "We have found that a night of meditation in the care of jailer Soyez invariably produces a change of attitude."

The inspector rose. "You have nothing further to say, I take it," he said.

"I do," Logan said. "Go screw yourself."

Logan got up and started for the narrow doorway that led into the rear of the jail. The man, Soyez, fell into step behind him. He could feel the man's excitement. He had already sized him up. With room to move, he would be easy enough to take. In close quarters, his raw strength would be rough, very rough. Soyez prodded Logan into the adjoining room and Logan felt his temper rise. That was good. He would need anger to hold out. He walked into the room and heard the door close behind him. Four empty cells lined the far wall. An old desk stood just off-center. A wooden chair on casters yawned emptily in front of it. A lone, green-shaded light bulb hung from the ceiling. The place smelled of urine and stale vomit and he saw a parade of big, fat *cucarachas* leisurely moving across the floor. He felt his right wrist seized, suddenly, and the coldness of metal. Soyez yanked Logan forward to one of the cells and clamped the other handcuff onto one of the bars. His smile was a sneer of triumph and he rested a heavy hand on the butt of his Police .38 and surveyed his prisoner.

"It would be so much easier to shoot you and simply say you tried to escape," he mused aloud. "But the inspector doesn't like that. He wants truth, confessions, trials."

"Confessions and trials, not truth," Logan muttered. The jailer's sneer had become a vicious grimace. "Outside the front door are two guards," he said. "But in here there will be only the two of us. By morning, you will confess."

The man was too insensitive to read the icy determination in Logan's eyes, the inflexible will reflected in his jaw. Soyez went to the desk, rolled aside the chair and opened a drawer to pull out a round, thick, hard-rubber truncheon. He turned to Logan, slapping it into his beefy palm. It made a dull, flat, menacing sound. Soyez knew the value of terror. Only Logan wasn't terrorized. The jailer advanced and raised his arm. When he brought it down in a sudden arc, Logan raised his free arm instinctively. Too late, he saw the man change direction with his blow and sweep in under his upraised arm. The truncheon slammed across his belly. Logan felt more than saw the second blow land across the back of his neck, knocking him forward to his knees. The handcuff around the cell bar slid down with him as he fell forward. Again the rubber truncheon came down, this time across the base of his spine and he felt himself cry out as the sharp slivers of pain shot up through his body. He swung his free arm around, caught one of the cell bars and started to pull himself up, kicking out blindly at the same time, only to hear the jailer's harsh laugh. The time, the truncheon landed hard against the backs of his knees and he felt himself collapse.

The truncheon came down again, and again, and now the man was beating a steady tattoo with it. Logan cast out with his one free arm but it was no more than a blind, futile gesture. Soyez used the truncheon skillfully, hitting those places where few marks would show. As the rubber truncheon landed hard against the small of his back, Logan steeled himself against waves of pain. He turned each agonizing blow into a hymn of revenge, fighting off the waves of nausea, concentrating on the murderous fury inside himself. He wondered how many men Soyez had beaten to death. I'm going to kill this sick, sadistic bastard, Logan told himself over and over, repeating the promise with each new blow. And then, suddenly, the blows stopped. He heard the jailer's voice.

"Only a beginning, my friend, only a sample."

Logan felt himself being uncuffed and flung into the cell. He was on the floor of the jail cell and heard the cell door clank shut behind him. He lay there, face down, thoughts moving through his mind, separate, disconnected bits of semiconsciousness. The stone floor was cold and the perspiration on his face gathered there in little droplets.

He let his eyes open into slits, taking a long moment to focus and adjust. He could see across the floor, through the cell bars, to where Soyez sat with his feet up on the desk. He saw the man lift up the rubber truncheon, push away from the desk and send himself and the little chair on casters rolling back across the floor to the opposite wall. The lean, hard man on the cell floor remained motionless but was forming a plan. He felt surging, icy fury gather, fill his pain-wracked body with new strength.

He lay there and waited and watched Soyez roll himself in the chair toward the cell. Then the man rose, pushing the chair away, and Logan saw the jailer's feet grow larger as he approached the cell, heard the sound of the man's voice calling to him. He remained motionless, as if dead. Soyez called again and then Logan heard the cell door being opened. He felt the man's big, beefy hands turning him over on his back, and he kept his body completely limp, holding his breath. On his back, seeing only through slitted eyes, he saw the blurred shape of the jailer bend down. As the man bent closer, Logan erupted, bringing his knee up sharply, feeling it smash up between the man's legs. Soyez let out a howl of pain, grabbed at himself, and Logan brought him down and was on him instantly, smashing a fist into the thick lips. The jailer tried to get an arm up but Logan drove his own forearm hard into the man's throat, hearing the sharp gasp of pain that followed. He brought his knee down again into the man's groin, smashed into Soyez's neck and then locked his fingers onto the jailer's throat. He clung there, pressing his body down hard onto the heavier man, digging his fingers deeply into the thick neck. Soyez flung his body about, trying to dislodge the lighter man, but Logan was fastened onto him like a limpet on a rock, unshakeable, his hands tightening slowly around the man's throat. Soyez's eyes grew wide with fear. His heaving motions grew more frantic, but Logan held his position and tightened his hands. His fingers were like steel claws, and Soyez was breathing in harsh, rasping draughts, clawing with his own hands at Logan's wrists. But he had already been robbed of strength and his motions grew weaker and weaker.

The struggle was fought in silence, and only the heaving, rolling, twisting movements of the battlers attested to its savagery. Logan thought briefly of all those who had come before him, of all the poor slobs Soyez had beaten, and he pressed down for the final few seconds. The man's heavy body suddenly went limp, the harsh breathing ended, and it was over. Logan unlocked his fingers with an effort, slowly massaging them.

He reached down and picked up the lifeless form and dragged it to the chair. Then he rolled the chair and its limp occupant over to the cell door. He took the keys from the dead jailer's pocket, entered the cell and slammed the door shut. Reaching out through the bars he locked the cell door from the outside. He took the keys and shoved them back into Soyez's pocket. Then, bracing himself on one leg, he pushed his foot through the space between the bars and sent the chair rolling on its casters across the floor to crash into the desk. Soyez's form toppled from the chair as it smashed into the desk and crumpled onto the floor, half-under the desk. Logan turned, lay down on the narrow cot at one side of the cell and went to sleep.

CHAPTER THREE

The commotion in the morning was almost worth the price of admission. The two outside guards found Soyez first when they came in to check their carbines before going off duty. They called the inspector, got him out of bed, and he rushed down to the jail. And there his jailer was, very, very dead, the keys to the cells in his pocket and Logan locked inside the cell. No one had come in or out, the guards swore, and Soyez had been clearly strangled to death. Logan stayed on the cot and only glanced up when the white suit of the inspector pressed against the cell bars.

"Of course, you know nothing about this, either," the man said, his lips pursed.

"Right again," Logan said from the cot. "I'm a heavy sleeper."

The inspector's eyes were narrowed, speculative, the eyes of a man who knows he's been had but doesn't know how.

"The man is dead, strangled to death, and there you are locked inside your cell some twenty-five feet away from his body," the inspector mused aloud. "It is what you call an *airtight alibi,* no?"

"It'll do," Logan said. He watched the inspector turn and stroll out of the room, past the men taking out Soyez's body in a canvas sack. The inspector returned fifteen minutes later. He unlocked the cell door.

"You have a visitor," he said, and hidden in his tone was a note of surprised respect.

"Oh, yeah?"

"You may speak to him out here." The inspector called to the adjoining room, *"Señor* Alvarez, in here, please." The inspector left the two men alone.

Logan's lean, lined face stayed impassive as he watched his visitor enter, a tall man, expensively clothed in a blue-gray silk suit, light blue shirt and diamond tie clip. The man reeked of confidence. He had olive skin, long sideburns and a straight nose.

"Buenos días," the man called Alvarez said. "You are not surprised to see me?"

"Not really," Logan said. "I just don't know whether to break you in half now or later. Where's your messenger boy?"

Alvarez smiled. "I decided to come myself," he said. "But let us not be unfriendly. We only did what we had to do. Your uncooperative attitude forced us to take steps."

"That was nothing. I can be a lot more uncooperative."

"So it seems," Alvarez smiled again. "The inspector told me of the most unusual death of his jailer. More and more I become pleased at selecting you and your boat, *Señor* Logan."

"Got to hell."

"You are no fool," Alvarez continued, his voice growing less charming. "You know, Soyez will be replaced by another of his kind. There will be more beatings. You could rot away here. You might even hang." He paused and smiled. "For the murder of the girl, of course."

Logan permitted himself a small grin.

"On the other hand," Alvarez went on, "I can have you out of here in five minutes and your boat released at once."

"You confessing to the chickie's murder?"

"Let us say I will provide information as to who the girl is and who killed her."

"Providing I agree to do that delicate job your boy spoke of."

"That is correct."

"Your boy offered me ten thousand," Logan said. "I want half of it in advance, certified check only."

Alvarez shook his head. "You are a most unique man, Logan," he said. "But I came prepared, suspecting as much."

"And that girl I had with me last night," Logan said. "I want her back aboard tonight. Straighten it out with her and tell her I'm waiting. Her name is Julie. Now let's get the hell out of this flea's paradise. You can tell me the rest on the boat."

"You boys go all the way to set up a frame, don't you?" Logan commented as he and Alvarez sat down on the *Urchin's* deck chairs. Logan had already scanned his boat with the eyes of a man who knows every inch of his woman and can instantly tell whether she's been touched or not.

"Do not feel too flattered," Alvarez answered. "We did not kill her. Her boy friend did that. We only borrowed her."

"Suppose you tell me what I do to earn my ten thousand?" Logan poured bonded bourbon for each, and Alvarez lifted his glass. *"Gracias,"* he said. "Your job is really very simple. You are merely to take someone someplace."

Logan's eyes told Alvarez he didn't believe anyone shelled out ten thousand for anything simple. "Cut the sales pitch or you can forget our agreement," he growled. "Just who the hell are you? Let's start with that."

"I represent the government of Peru," Alvarez said. "We are having a problem with a very dangerous, left-wing revolutionary group. They are active in the jungle mountains near the coast where it is difficult to pin them down. They have been led by a man of mystery named Panico. He is personally known to only a few people but he has been made into a legendary figure, a symbol of the revolutionary movement. Recently, some of our troops did engage a guerrilla force in pitched battle. We have reason to believe this Panico was killed in that encounter. But the revolutionary forces have denied this. They claim he is alive."

"Understandable," Logan said. "The death of a leader is often the death of a movement."

"Precisely," Alvarez went on. "We believe they have buried him in a little, remote village inland from the coast. We want you to take someone who knows Panico to the cemetery in that village. There, you will dig up the body and positive identification will be made, one way or another. It is very important to us that we know."

"Why the *Urchin* and me?" Logan asked. 'Why not just send someone else to do your grave-digging?"

"The guerrilla forces are thick in that area. They have people who would instantly spot and kill our men. But your boat is exactly the kind of tub that could conceivably be traveling up the Río Tinina to pick up hides or bark. You could get to the village with our agent."

"And after the body is identified as this Panico, or as somebody else, what then?"

"You bring our agent back, that is all."

"And Panico?"

"He stays. We only need him identified," Alvarez finished.

"That ten thousand," Logan said. "I want the whole thing in advance." He didn't say that because he felt that something about the whole story smelled. He didn't have to.

"Impossible!" Alvarez bristled. "Then there would be nothing to stop you from sailing away with our money."

"That's right. But I won't, and you know it."

Alvarez muttered under his breath but drew out four checks for twenty-five hundred each. Logan noted, as he stuffed them into his pocket, that both bore bank certification stamps.

"Where do I pick up your man? And when?"

"At the entrance to the harbor there is a red buoy," the Peruvian said. Logan nodded. "I know it," he added.

"At four o'clock this morning our agent will approach the buoy in a rowboat. A flashlight will signal with four flashes. You will answer with two sets of flashes. The rest of your instructions will come from our agent."

"Four o'clock, the red buoy," Logan repeated. Alvarez rose and handed him a slip of paper with a phone number written on it. "I can be reached at this number should you have any further questions," he said. He paused on the gangway and looked back at Logan.

"Tell me," he said. "How did you kill the inspector's man and lock yourself inside the cell?"

"I didn't kill him," Logan said. "Soyez ate some bad tortillas. Make sure the girl, Julie, is here tonight," Logan added. "Or your man's going to have a long wait around that red buoy."

He went down inside the forward cabin, stripping off his trousers and shirt as he went. The *Sea Urchin*, contrary to Alvarez's opinion, was both spacious and comfortable inside and he enjoyed the luxury of a shower. He still hurt plenty from where the big bastard had worked him over with that truncheon but that would pass. Purely physical pain always passes. It was the other kind that never went away, and for a moment the tall, lean man's eyes grew haunted. He stepped from the shower, towel in hand, and continued to dry himself as he reached into the pocket of his trousers and drew out the four checks. Wrapping the towel about his groin he sat down and pulled out the small writing board of the little desk built into the forward section of the cabin. He put three checks in an envelope and sent them to an account in his name in Key West. Then, the other check before him, he took out a sheet of notepaper. His dark probing eyes softened as he began to write, slowly, gracefully:

Sister Mary Angela
Mission of Mercy Sisters
Nairobi, Kenya

Dear Sister:

For you, to use as you need. Like all the others, it comes to you with the same thanks and the same memories. They stay with me, always just below the surface. Be sure to let me know if you transfer elsewhere.

With gratitude ... Logan

He put the check in with the letter, sealed the envelope, and thought briefly of the close link, as Henry James had put it, "between the things that help and the things that hurt." He shut out the flood of memories that threatened to engulf him and quickly dressed. On the quay, he strolled past fishermen bringing in their catch, tradesmen with pushcarts of fruit and vegetables, early-afternoon whores and a sprinkling of tourists. At the far end of the quay, beside a telephone booth, was a mailbox. He dropped both envelopes inside and turned, looking up at the sky. The air was heavy, thick and humid. It was the kind of weather that made seamen uncomfortable. It refused to point in any direction. It could just sit there or it could build up to vicious thunder squalls. He went back to the *Urchin* and checked out every compartment, every special piece of gear he had aboard, every spare part he kept in the spacious below-deck storage compartment. It was a procedure he undertook before any job. It made him feel better. The *Urchin* had cabins both forward and aft. He decided to give his passenger the aft one and he straightened it up. The night he had spent in jail had left him with a lot of rest to make up and he decided to take some of it. He went into the fore section and stretched out on one of the wall bunks. The heat and his own tired body let him go to sleep almost at once and when he finally woke it was nearly dark. He went up onto the deck, feeling refreshed but more unsatisfied than ever. He expected the girl. His lips tightened. If Alvarez thought he had been bluffing, he would find out how mistaken he'd been. He returned to the cabin for a moment, opened up a small liquor cabinet and made himself a Logan Special—bourbon, ice, dash of grenadine and bitters. He took it back on deck with him and sat down. Where the hell was the girl? He thought of Alvarez and how he still owed him plenty for framing him into taking that beating. It would serve Alvarez right if he just took off into the night. The Peruvian hadn't given him the whole truth, anyway. He could feel that in his bones. Two girls, young and long-legged, walked past along the quay and Logan watched their smooth, provocative legs moving along, slender stems going up into firm thighs that disappeared beneath their skirts, mockingly. Damn! Logan muttered and went below to fix himself another drink.

He came back on deck, feeling his mood growing blacker with every passing second. And then, walking beside the phone booth at the far end of the quay, passing beneath the lamplight, he saw her coming, black skirt and scoop-necked blouse. He waited, watching her as she neared and saw her pause at the gangway, then step onto it. His eyes lingered on the firm, young flesh of her thighs as she crossed the gangway and he passed the drink to her as she came aboard. She took it and pulled at it quickly, eager for its instant assurance. She was, as he'd remembered, young and eager and bouncy, despite her uncertainty. She took another long pull at the drink.

"Everything's all right, they told me," she said, getting a smile out. He cupped her chin in her hand.

"Everything's fine," he said, grinning at her. "Sit down."

He made her another drink, and one for himself, bringing them on deck.

"What was it all about?" she asked, hesitantly.

"Just somebody playing a joke on me," he answered, thinking how the answer wasn't really a lie. "Some people have a strange sense of humor."

"I'll say," she replied, draining her drink. They talked a while longer and laughed and he felt the desire stirring inside him as his eyes fastened on her small but upturned breasts, watching the way they moved under the satin blouse. The incompleteness of the night before had left its mark on the girl, too, he saw in her eyes as they searched his hungrily. Logan reached out a hand and put it on her arm. It acted like a door flung open, and in seconds she was in his arms, her warm, open mouth pressing upon his, lips working, tongue sending out messages of its own. His hands found her breasts, as soft as he'd remembered, and she thrust herself against him.

"I wanted to come back," she murmured. "You're something different. Something about you stays with a girl."

His answer was to send his tongue slowly revolving inside her mouth, and she moaned. He stopped, put his arm around her and led her below deck. He'd decided on the forward cabin this time, where the layout was different, and there would be no reminders. He turned off the lights and switched on the blowers. Cool air burst through the cabin. In the dim light, he saw her whip off her blouse, then her skirt. Pushing her back onto the bed, small but large enough for his purposes, he undid her bra and the soft breasts seemed to reach up for his lips. He lowered his head onto them, rolling his face in their softness, and then let his tongue trace small circles around their tips, first one and then the other, feeling each little tip rise under his touch. The girl was making small, eager sounds as he let his lips travel down over her body, across her abdomen, onto the softness of her rounded belly and then retrace their lambent path back to her straining breasts. She arched her back and he felt her legs under him opening, yawning, beckoning, and he answered, moving softly, gently.

He was with her, locked in the embrace of her legs, when his ears, always alert, like those of a cat, heard a sound, a faint movement on the deck. He tensed, holding himself still, listening, and he heard it again, a slurred footstep, and then he felt the girl grab at him.

"Don't stop," she gasped. "Damn it, don't stop now!" She pushed her belly upward against him frantically, intent only on pursuing the ecstacy nearly within her grasp. But Logan heard the step on the stairs and, in one swift motion, he pressed himself against the girl, grabbed her and rolled off the bed with her. They came apart only as they hit the floor and at the same instant the three shots resounded, crashing into the bed. Julie's scream was muffled against Logan's bare chest as he reached up under the mattress and yanked out the big Colt Python .357 magnum.

"¡Viva Camacho!" he heard the would-be killer shout as he appeared, framed in the doorway. The big-bore Colt Python erupted, firing two shots almost as one, and Logan saw the figure arch backward, seeming to leap into the air as the heavy slugs slammed into it. Logan, on his feet instantly, crossed the cabin in one lithe bound to stare down at the dead man sprawled across the two bottom steps of the companionway, "¡Viva Camacho!," he had yelled. Who the hell's Camacho? Logan asked himself. He stepped over the crumpled figure, grasped the man's shirt collar and pulled him onto the deck, taking care to keep him on his back so that the fast-spreading red stain wouldn't spill onto the deckboards. He looked up to see the girl, red satin blouse pulled over her, black skirt wrapped crookedly around her waist, edging out the companionway. She looked down at the dead man and up at Logan, her eyes round with fear.

"Wait," Logan said to her, but she shook her head as she edged past.

"No," she said. "Oh, no. I'm sorry but you got too many funny friends."

He watched her as she stumbled up onto the gangway, shot an apologetic glance back at him, and hurried on, pulling her skirt straight with one hand. Logan kicked the dead man in the head. "Bastard!" he said. 'Whoever the hell you are!"

He lifted the man by the back of his shirt and pushed him overboard, lowering the body over the side so it wouldn't land with a noisy splash. It would, he knew, float around the cove until someone discovered it in the morning. He went below, put his clothes back on and hurried onto the quay. It was just past midnight, his watch told him, and he went to the phone booth at the end of the quay. He called the number Alvarez had given him and heard the man's voice snap awake as he identified himself.

"What happened?" Alvarez asked.

"That's what I'd like to know. This more of your stuff?" he finished.

"No, no, not at all," Alvarez said. "They had me watched, I know, but I thought we took care of that. Apparently, they sent someone else who saw me go aboard your boat. I suggest you sail for the red buoy at once and wait there. The man you killed may have had others with him."

"Who the hell is Camacho?" Logan asked. "I thought you said their leader was Panico."

"I do not know any Camacho," Alvarez said but Logan caught a small pause in the man's voice. He's lying, Logan told himself. He hung up. He was getting more curious himself, now. He'd had his ass beaten in a crummy little cell, and just missed getting three slugs in the back, and he hadn't even begun the job yet. The ten thousand's beginning to look like bargain rates, he told himself. Back aboard the *Sea Urchin* he started the engine and let the twin V-12 diesels purr quietly while he cast off bow and stern lines. Then, nosing the boat out into the cove, he headed for the wide mouth of the harbor in the blackness of the hot, humid, thick-aired night.

"Let's go, honey," he said, quietly. "Let's find the little red buoy. Like the girl said, I've got too many funny friends around here."

CHAPTER FOUR

Logan heard the steady clang of the red buoy as he neared it, and he used his flashlight to study the chart in his hand. The reefs were to the right of the buoy he noted on the chart, where the harbor curved in a slow arc. The chart told him he had more then enough spare water around the buoy and, cutting his engine speed, he began to execute lazy circles around the clanging signal. His body once more seethed with restlessness as he thought of the girl's soft breasts. He felt like a starving man who'd sat down to a banquet only to have it yanked away. He shifted in the seat and patted the big Colt Python he'd stuck into his belt. He'd hoped for a moon but instead a steady, fine rain began to fall about three o'clock, which added to the blackness of the night. He was running without lights, and that was always dangerous. Coastal patrol cruisers were his main concern. These waters were a haven for smuggling contraband of all kinds and the police coastal cruisers had a habit of running without fights, too, as they searched for smugglers. A boat with running lights circling the red buoy for three hours would surely attract attention, probably from shore patrols, too. So he had opted for no lights, and now he peered into the moonless night searching for any black bulks that might loom up.

It was nearly four when he stopped circling and headed upwind of the buoy, cut the powerful engines and let the boat slowly drift back toward the buoy. His eyes swept the blackness and his ears were turned for the faintest sound. Only the soft slap of the sea against the hull broke the silence. He leaned his head out of the pilot house window and let the soft rain cool his face. Then, suddenly, he heard another sound, the faint scrape of an oar against the metal side of a boat. He slowed his sweep of the inky blackness and then, to the right, saw the flash, followed by three more. He waited and let the light flash four times again before answering. Then he blinked his flash twice, and twice again, in the answering signal. He'd just switched off his flash when he heard the dull, ominous sound, a powerful engine running at low speed. He spun around and, squinting through the fine rain, was able to pick out the black bulk of another vessel off the port bow. He traced the line of the high prow, high forward cabin and low stem, and knew at once the vessel was a coastal patrol boat. It was also plain that they'd seen the *Urchin's* bulk and were heading for her.

Logan peered to the other side and saw the rowboat materializing through the rain, the lone occupant rowing furiously, having also heard the patrol boat's engines. He moved fast, tossing a line over the side of the *Sea Urchin* and then, racing back to the wheel, kicked over the port engine. It sent the boat skittering a few feet sideways through the water as he yanked at the wheel, bringing it closer to the frantic oarsman. Logan heard the night come alive with the deep, throaty sound of the patrol cruiser's horn and he saw the boat's running lights snap on. But the rower had reached the side of the *Urchin* and grasped the line. With Logan pulling on it, the figure clambered up the side of the boat. Logan glimpsed a loose jacket, trousers and a floppy oilskin hat pulled low over the face. But he also saw smooth cheeks, an unlined face. It was no more than a kid, a small canvas bag slung over his shoulder.

"Get down," Logan commanded. He left the crouched figure with the big oilskin hat and raced below into the forward cabin.

He had to work fast. The patrol boat would switch its searchlight on any second, he knew. He reached up to the top edge of what seemed the plain wall siding of the cabin and, running his fingers along the top, pulled down hard. The side of the wall opened up to reveal a hidden alcove, six feet long by nearly three feet wide. He left it open and raced back onto the deck.

"Inside the forward cabin," he said to the figure crouched at the rail. "Climb into the wall and pull the side back up with you."

He went to the wheel, a plan already formed in his mind. He didn't want any trouble with the coastal patrol, no dawn chases that he might or might not win. He'd let them come aboard, look around and then tell them he had been running without lights because he'd had generator trouble. Maybe they'd give him a jaundiced eye, but they would have to take his word for it. He'd get a reprimand, or possibly a summons, and that would be it. He had started to swing the *Urchin* around when the powerful searchlight beam opened up the night, a wide, blue-white finger probing the dark. It caught the pilot house at once and Logan waved and throttled the engine. He followed the beam of light as it swung down to the forward deck, moved slowly, then stopped as it illumined the small figure crouched at the gunwale.

"*Sonofabitch!*" Logan exploded, surprise and fury matching each other. "Dammit to hell!" He had just ended his second oath when the shots erupted, cracking the night and shattering the patrol boat's searchlight. Logan's hands clenched in helpless rage and he heard the angry voices from the cruiser as the light went out.

"That did it!" Logan swore, and he gunned the engines at once. Had it not been necessary for him to handle the *Urchin*, he'd have been on deck, strangling the crouching figure by the rail. There was no chance of playing it cool, now, and he knew that aboard the coastal patrol boat they were yanking the cover from their deck gun, probably a 20 mm machine gun. Logan saw them swinging around to bring their aft light into play, and as the light came on, he heard another fusillade of shots and the light went dark at once. A burst of machine gun fire whistled over the roof of the pilot house. He opened the throttle to full and kicked the rudder to port. The *Urchin* turned and leaped forward like a skittish sea horse, the powerful propellers grabbing at the water below. He assumed the coastal patrol was radioing for help, figuring he'd try to put in at one of the nearby coves. He straightened out the wheel and sent the *Urchin* surging forward in a shower of salt spray. The clouds and rain were holding off the first early streaks of dawn, and he was grateful for that. They sent another spray of shots after him but he had opened water between them, and until they closed it, he wasn't worried about the gunfire. The *Urchin* moved with surprising speed, surprising to anyone watching her, that was. The plowhorse was running like a thoroughbred. But to Logan there was little surprise. He knew what she could do. But he also knew that, given enough time, the coastal patrol boat would probably eat its way up to her if only because its streamlined prow offered less water resistance.

He opened the throttle a few notches more, just about all she had, and he glanced forward at the deck. His passenger had gone below and Logan's lips tightened in a surge of fury. Light was beginning to tint the sky, gray, murky light, but still fight. If they were able to get his name and number, they'd have every harbor master in every stinking cove alerted. Logan leaned his head out the window, peering forward, and suddenly he swung the *Urchin* to starboard. A fogbank was spreading across the water, low and wide, plenty wide enough in which to get lost. He couldn't tell how long it was. He took a fast bearing, threw a glance at the chart, veered back to port a little, and went into the fogbank at full speed, hoping no one else was hiding inside it. The fog closed around the boat at once and muffled the deep roar of its engines. He was sitting alone in a disembodied pilot house, with no bow and stern to his boat as the fog closed its pink-gray blanket around him. Logan cut the engines to half-speed and put on the autopilot. He couldn't see anything so he turned on the radar and watched the scope for a few moments. Everything seemed to be clear ahead. He slipped from the pilot's seat and headed for the companionway, the fury within taking a renewed lease with each step. The youth was bent over inside the cabin, rummaging through the canvas bag, his back to the door. Logan's foot lashed into his behind and the figure flew headlong across the small cabin.

"On my boat you do as I say," Logan roared. The youth hit the bunk, went sprawling across it, and the oilskin hat flew off. Logan, crossing after the figure quickly, halted as a cascade of jet black hair came tumbling down and the figure turned around.

"I'll be damned!" Logan cursed. "A girl!" He saw her eyes, as black as her hair, lose some of their fury as she looked up at him. She was not only a girl but a beautiful one, with long black hair framing a heart-shaped face, straight nose and full, sensuous lips. Lying on her back half-across the bunk, her breasts swelled and she pushed herself upright.

"They didn't tell you?" she asked.

"Not a goddamn word."

"Does it make so much difference?" He felt his blood starting to boil over.

"Yes, it makes a difference. I agreed to get someone to a village, not to be a wetnurse to some crazy chickie."

"You won't be a wetnurse to me," she snapped. "Or didn't you see me take care of that coastal patrol boat?"

"I saw you almost get us both arrested. Why didn't you get the hell down?"

"I thought I'd be more help on deck."

"On my boat I do the thinking. You give me a hard time and I'll kick your little ass right over the side."

Logan turned and strode from the cabin. On deck, he checked the radar screen. He cut off the engines. There was no sound but the sound of her following him. She stood at the rail.

"They're waiting back there for us to come out," she said.

"Yes, but we're going on through and out the other end."

He watched her face closely but saw only a small, enigmatic smile.

"You're supposed to tell me where we go from here."

"Down the coast of Peru, just above the Río Huarmey, we'll come to a small inlet, the mouth of the Tinina River. We go up the Tinina, far upriver, to a little village called Quechayo."

Logan pulled a chart from the compartment just below the wheel and studied it for a moment. "No problem getting to the Tinina," he said. "You know the country from there?"

"Not really," she answered. "We'll be on our own once we start upriver."

They were starting to come out of the bank and he switched off the radar, turned on the engines and peered through the now patchy wisps of vapor. The sun was out and the yellowness of it fought through the fog and then, suddenly, they were out of the fog into morning sun.

'What's your name?" Logan thought to ask.

"Ariana," she said. "Ariana dos Vayez. You, I know, are called Logan."

Logan saw that they were in clear waters and he headed due south through the long swells of the Pacific. He set a course that would take him far enough off shore to skirt the bulge where Ecuador jutted out into the Pacific. He watched the girl at the rail. Her figure was long, slender, and the blue-jeans clung to her narrow hips. Finishing school, Logan muttered to himself. Then some fancy girl's college. It always showed in the way they moved, in a certain arrogance of the body. She was used to money, to good things. He put on the autopilot and went down to the deck.

"Where'd you learn English?"

"In America," she said. "I went to school there, finishing school. And in Switzerland."

"I don't like being tricked," he said. "And I don't like operating in the dark. How do you fit into this bit?"

"I dated Panico when we were in college," she said. 'I'm one of the few people who know him well enough to identify him. Among those on our side, that is."

"What's your side?"

"I work for the Peruvian Government. Like *Señor* Alvarez. Normally, I work in the Diplomatic offices. They asked me to do this and I agreed."

Logan tinned her answers over in his mind. He wasn't at all sure he believed her. There were soft spots, just as there had been with Alvarez. South American governments didn't go in for using women in sensitive areas. He tabled her answers for the time being and turned to her. A sea wind blew the red jersey against her breasts, outlining the round undersides of them and the rising, upturned tips. Logan felt the unsatisfied hunger inside himself rise like a dull ache.

"I'm going below for some sleep," he said, gruffly. They were in open waters and any vessels would be able to see them. The autopilot would hold their course well enough till he came back. And he was tired. But, as he went below, he knew it was not tiredness alone that sent him to the forward cabin.

"You have the aft cabin," he called back to the girl. He felt her eyes watching him as he disappeared below decks. He undressed and stretched out on the bunk. A slow smile moved across his lips. Maybe the trip would have its own rewards. If she wanted to play games he'd play, too. Only she'd find out he played for keeps. Ariana. The name moved across his mind. An unusual name. An unusual girl. He went to sleep.

CHAPTER FIVE

The midday sun was hot and Ariana was on the foredeck when Logan emerged from the cabin. In deep pink shorts and a turquoise blouse, she rose on one elbow as he appeared. Her legs, he saw at once, were long, lithe and slowly curving, and they moved lazily as she stirred. Her jet-black hair hung loosely, almost to the middle of her back, and her onyx eyes reflected amusement as she saw the open admiration in his eyes. Logan caught the note of anticipation in her eyes as he came toward her. She was used to being admired and had the honesty to openly enjoy it. Logan walked past her, glanced again at her, and gazed out across the sea. They were going before a good current and making time, he noted.

"No comment?" he heard the girl say mockingly. He turned and looked down at her, his face impassive.

"Do you need one?" he asked.

"No, but it's always nice to get one."

"All right, you're beautiful," he said, flatly.

"I've never heard a compliment sound less like one."

"It was a statement of fact. Someone said beauty is its own excuse. It doesn't need compliments."

"Maybe beauty doesn't but girls do."

He went up the side of the deck, pulled himself onto the small ledge surrounding the pilot house and went to the wheel. He was checking out his instruments, engine synchrometer, fuel oil pressure, tachometer when she appeared in the doorway.

"Who are you, Logan?" she asked, watching the slow smile crease the man's face as he continued to check the gauges in front of him.

"Nobody. Everybody," he said. "A sea-going bum. Arms and legs for hire."

"A sea-going bum who can quote the poets." She moved up and sat down on the narrow seat beside the port window.

"You're no sea-going bum," she said. "You're running away from something."

He laughed. "Sorry, honey," he said. "I hate to disappoint you but I'm not on anybody's wanted list. Nobody's after me. No cops, no governments, nobody."

"Maybe just yourself."

"How are you at making lunch?" he changed the subject.

"Pretty good."

"The galley is forward," he said. "The refrigerator and the freezer are well stocked. You're on your own."

"Lunch coming up," she said and hurried out of the pilot house. He watched her go, her small, compact rear moving gracefully with every step. He checked the course, made a few corrections, reset the autopilot and went below. He came up with a tray, ice, glasses and bourbon just as Ariana emerged from the galley. She had made bacon and lettuce sandwiches on toast and not even burned the bread. They sat on the deck, under the bright Pacific sun, and ate and he saw that she could enjoy the good warmth of the best bourbon and he found himself wondering again about her. Maybe she did work for the Peruvian Government in the Diplomatic offices but she was no office girl, no earnest little file clerk. She was a girl used to having what she wanted, used to looking down, not up, to people. It was in every gesture of her, in the way she tossed her head, in the way her eyes flashed with that touch of controlled arrogance. She caught the speculative look of his eyes as he watched her and smiled.

"What are you thinking, Logan?"

"That you dress up the *Urchin*," he lied, blandly. She laughed and the laugh said that she knew he had merely tossed her a bone and not his thoughts.

"You are like your boat," she said. "Deceptive. The inside is very different from the outside. And you hide the inside purposely. What do you think about when you're sailing alone?"

"Nothing I just stare out at the ocean," Logan said, annoyance coloring his voice. "Don't keep making something out of me that I'm not. I'm a drifter. I like to do nothing and do it slowly. I leave thinking to other people."

She made a face. "Baloney. You think all the time, too much, probably."

Logan felt his temper rise. Her perception and intuition were a disturbing combination and her fast, sharp probes were more than merely annoying. In fact, he decided, she was very bothersome all the way through.

"How'd you like to be locked in your cabin?" he growled.

"I wouldn't. Give me some work to do," she said, suddenly, eagerly. Logan seized the thought at once. It would keep her busy and out of his way while he checked out the sluggishness of the bilge pumps.

"There are rags and there is polish in the aft port closet," he said. "You can do the deck fittings."

She hurried down to get her equipment. Logan went below and pulled up the engine hatch cover. He'd keep plenty busy with the pumps...

But by the day's end, the good idea was still good, only it hadn't really worked. He had fixed the pumps quickly, too quickly, and with too much time left to watch Ariana. She polished and cleaned with the carefree joy of someone who doesn't normally have to work and who can afford to make work a fun game. And every curve and bend of her body was a delight to watch. By dinner time she was back in the galley, broiling steaks from the freezer, and Logan's angry restlessness had grown worse. His calculations told him they'd passed Colombia and were proceeding along the coast of Ecuador. He went into his cabin, showered and put on a fresh, white shirt. When he returned to the deck she had the small trays out, the steaks ready, and had changed into deep blue slacks and a white halter top, bare-midriffed. Logan's lips pressed together in a tight line.

He brought up a bottle of bourbon and made Logan Specials to go with the steaks. Dinner was fun and her vitality and wit were on a par with her beauty. She was having too much fun to notice the determined decision in the lean man's eyes. Darkness came over the Pacific and Logan switched on the running lights. They cast a low glow over the deck. The half-moon did the rest and the more he watched and listened to her, the more convinced he became that there was more to her being there, on his boat, then he'd been told. Her ability to describe a place, an event, an occurrence with complete detail seemed to disappear whenever he brought up anything concerning her mission. Her reaction to his questions about Panico stayed in his mind.

"What did this character Panico look like when you dated him?" he had asked.

"Very ordinary looking," she'd answered and started onto something else. But he'd pressed further.

"Was he blond, red-haired, dark?"

"His hair was just an everyday color," she said, a small, nervous frown crossing her face. She was being purposely evasive, unwilling to be pinned down about the man. Why? he asked himself, and came up with no answers.

"What if he had all his hair cut off and raised a mustache?" Logan probed. "Would you still be able to identify him?"

"I'll be able to make the identification," she said and closed off the subject. It had gone the same way when he tried to get her to talk about her work at the Embassy. She gave more fast, evasive answers that left his mind completely unsatisfied. She was a beautiful girl playing games. How many games, and what they were about, he didn't know. He only knew he was about to put a stop to one of them. He got up, drained his drink, and went over to her. He saw her eyes maintain their veiled, amused confidence. That was just as well, he knew, because there would be no stopping, no turning aside. His body would refuse to obey. The need that had been denied him twice now focused on this lovely, raven-haired creature in front of him. He put a hand on the back of her neck and felt the soft, wispy hairs there. He ran his hand partially down her back, and then lifted her to her feet. She rose to meet his lips, her mouth opening just a little. But his own hunger had burst loose and he pressed his mouth on hers, forcing his tongue into the warm, wetness of her mouth, darting, circling, anticipating further pleasures. She managed to pull away and tried to slip from his arms but he held her still. He yanked her head around and again pressed into the open, red invitation, this time feeling her own tongue answer in short, quick motions, like a bird taking flight.

"No, Logan!" she gasped as his hand fell on her breast and she clasped her own hand over his. But she didn't pull his away and her eyes were searching his, troubled, uncertain. Conflicting desires, were raging inside Ariana, he knew, and he gave some of them a little helpful push. He pulled the string of her halter and it fell from her and his hand was against her breast, pressing into the warm, vibrant flesh. Her body stiffened as she tried to hold back the pleasure she felt at his touch. But it was a useless gesture and suddenly her body pressed forward, her breast pushing itself into his palm. Her lips were hungry against his. He lifted her up and the halter fell off completely and he gazed down at the softly rounded breasts, cream-white gifts waiting for his lips. Ariana's head lay against his shoulder and she was making small sounds of protest but they were meant to be disregarded. He carried her to the cabin below and on the fold-out bed his lips fastened on the smooth tips of her breasts, caressing them with his tongue until the small, pink tips lifted in gratification and he moved his lips around the firm softness, the deep fullness of her chest. He let his hands pull down the slacks and move over the rise of her hips, across her flat belly, down to the exciting little mound of softness that waited for his touch.

As he moved across her, Ariana gave a cry of release that sprang from some hidden place and she threw herself upon him, rubbing herself against him, her hands clutching, caressing, stroking, and he matched her wild abandon, touching the wellsprings of passion she cried out for him to touch. Her lips sought every part of his body and she moved up and down the strong, oak-tree muscles of his frame, crying little cries of ecstasy and desire and when he pressed her back and thrust himself fully into her, she tossed her head from side to side and her fingers dug into him with a rapture more than she could contain. Higher and higher she reached with her body, half-crying, half-laughing, her little fists pounding against the bed as the tall, lean man carried her beyond being, beyond thinking, beyond feeling, to a place where there was only knowing.

"Logan!" she screamed the word. *"Oh, God, Logan!"* and as her body went steel-wire taut he went deeply into her and her neck arched backward, her mouth opened and the scream that

came was one of total surrender. He fell back onto the bed, keeping him with her until the world became real again. Logan gently massaged her breast until her regular breathing indicated she had relaxed. Only then did he pull away and lay beside her, feeling the accusation in her black eyes.

"I didn't want this," she said quietly, almost hesitantly.

"Didn't you?"

"Not tonight, not so soon."

"You wanted to play some more," Logan said, his voice cold. "Till you could decide when or if. You're used to having things your way. But I'm not one of the crowd."

"I know that," she said. "I saw that the first minute we met. You're different."

"And you liked that," he said. "But different things are often dangerous."

"I just found that out."

"Are you sorry?" He got to his feet and looked down at her, letting her drink in his nakedness. She turned away. "I don't know," she said quietly.

Logan's laugh was hard and short. "Tell me when you find out," he said, biting the words. He took his clothes and dressed on deck and his smile was thin. There were games she still had to play, he was certain. But there'd be one less now. He took the wheel of the boat and turned toward shore to find an inlet to anchor for the night. In a mile or so he spotted a small pocket and fitted the *Urchin* inside it. He dropped anchor, waited to make sure it was holding, and then turned off all but the white fight on the forward mast. He went to his cabin and stretched out, letting the sea wind through the porthole move across his naked body. He would sleep well, he knew. The hunger within him had been satisfied. Though Ariana had been so much more of everything then he'd expected that, in a strange way, she'd sharpened as well as satisfied his hunger. He thought of her cream-white body and the blackness of her hair. She could be everything to someone, sometime. But he was beyond those things, and as sleep drew a curtain over his mind, he wondered if he would ever care again about anyone. Nothing was impossible. But some things were highly improbable.

CHAPTER SIX

Bright hot sun made bearable by the sea winds, the deep blue of the Pacific a rolling carpet. That was morning and Logan made coffee and got under way early, once again staying far offshore. By noon, according to his charts, they'd be moving along the coast of Peru. He settled himself at the wheel. A helmsman, playing the wheel, could always make better time than the automatic pilot, and time had become important again to him. He wanted to do the job, get finished with it, and be on his way. Ariana was staying in her cabin, and that was good. Whatever had brought her into this strange and dirty business, were hers to wrestle with. He wouldn't get involved beyond the needs of his agreement. Involvements were something he'd ended long ago. He turned on the ship's radio, picked up a station, and settled down to concentrate on his job.

Ariana dos Vayez heard the man on the deck above and held her arms tightly across her breasts. She had put on a loose, rayon blouse and the pink shorts, and she could still feel the touch of his hands on her, the tingling of her body as he moved his lips across it. She had asked herself over and over all day why it had happened the way it had. It wasn't enough to blame the commonplace things, the soft Pacific night, the cool wind, the lulling swell of the waters. It wasn't even honest to blame the compelling looks of the man, the dangerous hardness about him that reached out and grabbed at you. She had wanted him, with a kind of wanting she had never experienced before. And when he had taken her, it was something she had never known could exist in just that way. She was on this boat to do something that had to be done, because she was the only one that could be trusted. She wasn't here to become involved with a strange and distant man. She had met many men, in her own country and in those lands where she had gone to school, but none like Logan. She had known men who refused to compromise and those who did nothing else. She had known men who were cold and men who were warm. She had known men who believed in honor and those who didn't even know the word. Honor, the word moved across her mind. It was a big word in her country, in most places, probably. But she wasn't sure anymore if it meant the same thing to all men. She wasn't even sure where honor really began, and ended, any longer. Very often it seemed that honor was really no more than which was best for you. She wasn't really sure of much anymore, except that you did what you did because you had to do it. You were brought up a certain way. You got used to certain things. You became part of a particular world, and it all decided what you did from there on.

The past really owns the future, Ariana told herself, at least for most of the world. Perhaps that was what was so intriguing about this lean, hard man and his deceptively funny little boat. He owned himself. He was one of the few who refused to let the past own the future. Of course there had been a past, that was clear, and it had left its mark. But only its mark, not its franchise. Ariana heard him go into the galley for coffee. He went back to the wheel as she traced his footsteps and fought down the urge to rush up on deck. It would be worth it if she could make him a part of her world, worth it for them both. A man like that could bring not only strength to her life but give her world a definition it needed. And she could give him material pleasures and comforts. Maybe, she mused idly, maybe. She would have to get over wanting him as much as she did. That made her position much weaker. But, she asked herself quickly, could she meet this man on his own terms? Was that the impossible thing about him that gave him the strangely compelling strength he had, the fact that his terms were his and his alone? She gazed out of the porthole. The sea flowed past, the sun-speckled surface somehow reflecting the terrible strength below, very much like the man at the wheel over her head.

Logan watched the coast of Peru grow larger as he piloted the *Sea Urchin* inshore. The afternoon sun had moved across the horizon and he scanned his chart closely. The mouth of the Tinina River was poorly marked and he estimated they would near it just before nightfall. It was time the girl started doing her job, which included the decisions on entering the river. He called to her, his voice flat, emotionless.

"Ariana. Get out here. We have to talk," he said, and heard the sounds of her moving about, then coming up the companionway. He watched the cascade of jet-black hair emerge and her eyes, and there were resentment, hostility and uncertainty in them. He could almost feel the turbulence of her and once again he found his eyes on the thrusting mounds of her breasts. They seemed to rise and swell as she walked up the few steps to the pilot house. He took his eyes from them and the girl's face and gazed out over the water as he spoke to her

"By night we'll be at the mouth of the Tinina," he said. "It's your show from there. I'm only the chauffeur. Do we start upriver or anchor and wait for morning?"

"Anchor," Ariana said. "The Tinina is tricky and winding. I don't know it that well. I only know it'll be hard enough by day "

"All right," Logan said "You can go back down below."

"No!" the girl said the one word with enough vehemence to surprise herself. "I … I want to talk about last night I want to explain."

Logan kept his eyes straight ahead, peering over the long blue swells. "There's nothing to explain," he said, flatly. "You wanted it to happen and it happened. That's all."

"No, that's not all," she said, angrily. "I'm no tramp."

"Anyone say you were?" he countered. "You want to explain to yourself," he said.

He saw the black fire shoot from her eyes, saw her swing in fury and he caught her wrist with one hand. He bent her body backward and she gasped. The buttons of the blouse came open and the rounds swell of her breasts emerged. She had nothing on beneath the blouse. He pressed his mouth on hers and felt her quiver and then she was kissing him back, lips open, tongue searching for his. He let go of her wrist and her hand flew against his chest, clutching his shirt, her fingers working on the muscled hardness of his skin. Suddenly, angrily, she tore away from him and stood back, her eyes boring into his.

"God, what is it about you?" she said, a question that was more of a statement than a question. "I don't want this, not this way, and yet I want you so bad it hurts."

"An unsolicited testimonial," Logan said, his grin hard, his eyes narrowed. She had gathered herself together and the anger in her had taken command.

"You never let up, do you?" she said.

"It's your comer. You put yourself in it."

"And you had nothing to do with it, I suppose," she snapped.

"Only a little," he said. "I just held up a mirror."

"That's how you get your kicks," she bit out.

Logan shrugged. "People shouldn't have hiding places," he said. "It makes them dishonest with themselves and then with each other. I make them face themselves. And that's important, even if they refuse to admit it."

She wanted to hit out at him to avoid the truth of what he was saying. She wanted to find a vulnerable spot and in so doing only exposed her own vulnerability.

"Why don't you try facing yourself?" she cast out, almost desperately. He caught her wrist again and pulled her to him.

"No problem, honey," he said through clenched teeth. "I want you again, tonight, before we start up that damned river. I want you and you want me. You don't want to want me but you do. You still want to play games." He thrust a hand up under the loose blouse and closed it over her round breast and she lifted her head and closed her eyes.

"Tonight, later," he said. "You'll be waiting for me and I'll come." He withdrew his hand and Ariana stepped backward, her eyes troubled, almost frightened. She turned and ran out of the pilot house and she heard the man's short, angry laugh.

Logan put his thoughts on following the curves of the Peruvian coastline. He passed a few fishing boats, mostly one and two-man operations. The full, lush foliage of the coastline told him of the country he'd be pushing through, heavy, over-grown, hot. He had slowed to half-throttle and he kept one eye on the lowering sun, one on the chart. The sun had just touched the distant line of the horizon and started to flatten out behind it when he reached the mouth of the Tinina River, a crack in the green wall of the coastline. He cruised past it, swung around and came by again. A small village graced the mouth of the river, mostly shacks, a few somewhat sturdier wooden houses. Canoes, small hand-rowed fishing craft, a few with outboard motors, and a shallow river barge made up the villlage waterfront. He found a spot just outside the mouth of the river and dropped anchor. By the time he'd made the *Urchin* secure for the night, darkness had closed down on the boat. He went below and made himself a Logan Special, took it on the deck and sipped it. He was taking his time, but he knew it was a double-edged sword, for his groin ached for the luscious creature in the cabin. He drained the drink and went down below, pushing open the cabin door. Ariana was still in the blouse and deep pink shorts, looking at him as he filled the doorway, legs curled up beneath her on the fold-out bed. He walked toward her, taking in the absolute beauty of the raven hair framing her cream-white skin. She waited till he was standing in front of her.

"I looked into one of those mirrors of yours," she said. "And I don't want what you want."

"Look again," Logan growled. "You'll see a damned liar."

He grabbed her by the back of the neck and yanked her head up. Her eyes grew blacker and her breath was deep, hard. He saw her lips move, her tongue flick out to wet them, and her mouth open before she said the one word.

"Bastard," she gasped and flew against him, her arms wrapping around his neck in a fervent grip. He forced her back onto the bed and felt the blouse come undone and his lips were on her breasts, moving on them, rapturously massaging their small, pink tips. Her hands were pushing against his trousers, taking them down over his hips so she could clutch him to her and she cried out in small, animal sounds of pure desire.

Dimly, she heard the sound of a mirror shattering.

Once more, he found the wild passion that was part of this gorgeous girl, but this time, she was more eager to make love to him. Her hand holding him stroked and smoothed and pressed and she moved her mouth across his body like a hungry little bird. The tall, lean man's face relaxed under the pleasures of her mouth, her circling, caressing tongue and he knew she was trying to say something with her body that words could not say. He reached down, lifted her head up to his and moved atop her. He would be less savage with her tonight, less savage but just as complete. The boat moved up and down slowly in the rhythm of the waves and Logan, tuning his own movements to it, brought Ariana to that wild moment when it seemed the world must explode. But still he delayed the explosion and once again she knew that feeling of transport, of pure and utter unbearable ecstacy. Her lovely breasts rose and fell and her gasping cries grew more and more intense. Once again he saw her pound her fists into the bed, saw her black hair fly as she tossed her head from side to side, and she cried out in her own tongue and in English. Then, with a tremendous thrust of her hips, there was no more time to delay, and the inner explosion of rapture tore through her body and she clutched at Logan, half-moaning, half-sobbing until slowly she relaxed. He lay down, half-atop her, resting his head on her breasts and she cradled him there. Finally, her even, steady breathing told him she'd fallen asleep and he moved his head from the wonderful softness of her breasts. He gazed at her. Sleep revealed more clearly the delicate lines of her heart-shaped face, her small wrists and fine-boned body, a body used to the best. And once again he had to wonder why this girl had taken on this strange task. It didn't add up.

He got to his feet and went on deck. He didn't know why but a strange sadness had gripped him, as if their lovemaking had been more of an end than a beginning. Somehow, he had the strangest feeling that, for all his having reached her so completely, he and this raven-haired girl would part bitterly. A small smile crossed his face. With a few it hadn't been bitter, he recalled, only bitter-sweet. But this girl, this creature of evasions and hidden pieces, still had to fit the pieces into a whole and he had the feeling that when she did, they wouldn't fit right, not for him. He lay down on the hardness of the deck and slept there.

CHAPTER SEVEN

Logan didn't know which hit him first, the thick, heavy-aired heat as he nosed the *Urchin* into the Tinina or the narrowness of the winding ribbon that stretched out ahead of him. The minute he'd entered the mouth of the river the heat had fallen onto them like an invisible curtain. The cooling winds of the Pacific swept by the river's mouth, refusing to extend even a probing finger of air into it. Logan moved the *Urchin* slowly past the ramshackle buildings that were clustered on both banks. He saw a man in a peaked and braided cap set out in a craft with a small outboard and a tillerman and he slowed the *Urchin* still further. The man was a town official, perhaps out to make his usual show of status for the people. Perhaps not. Ariana was below decks but watching through the porthole, he knew. It had already been decided that she would stay strictly out of sight. He had shown her how to pull down the wall siding and climb into the alcove at the first sound of anyone coming aboard. The little craft swung alongside the *Urchin* and the man in the cap called to Logan.

"Buenos días" Logan saw the notepad and pencil in his hand. "I am the river traffic master. May I have the name of your boat and your destination?"

A river traffic master on a stinkin' little river like this? Logan asked himself the question silently. Yet it was possible, he knew. These minor officials invented titles for themselves and duties for which they could collect extra pay.

"*Sea Urchin,*" Logan said. "I'm going upriver as far as I can go."

"Your business?" the man asked and Logan saw his eyes move up and down the length of the *Urchin's* paint-chipped hull.

"Hides and bark, and anything I can buy for a good price and sell for a better one."

The official touched his cap and pushed away. Logan gunned the *Urchin* and the boat responded at once. He grinned back at the craft, rocking precariously in the sudden rush of his wake. He had been gone from the village for almost a half hour before he slid open the small hatch in the floor of the pilot house. It let him look down into the passageway between the forward and aft sections of the boat and he saw Ariana appear at once, stepping up on the ladder to poke her head out of the hatch opening in the floor.

"What did you think, back there?" she asked.

"I think he was legitimate," Logan said. "But I wish I knew for sure." The girl's lovely face was passive and told him nothing. "These guerrillas," he said. "You think they'll really be watching for us? ... for someone?"

"Three of our people have been killed trying to get into Quechayo by land," she said quietly, and Logan's left eyebrow rose.

"Then you be sure and keep your ass out of sight during daylight," he said. "Then they can watch all they want and all they'll see is the *Urchin* and me moving upriver."

"I'll get lunch for us soon," she said. "This is fun in a way, isn't it?" She flashed him a little-girl smile of enthusiasm and disappeared. She didn't appear again till she came up with sandwiches and a can of beer. He steered with one hand and ate with the other. She stood on the ladder, her head and shoulders through the hatchway opening, her plate on the floor of the pilot house. Logan took off his shirt and sat at the wheel stripped to the waist. The heavy air lay like a blanket, oppressive, cloying, stealing energy in huge handfuls. The Tinina River was not only shallow, with shifting sandbars, but dotted with small islands in the center which necessitated skirting them along a needle-thin channel. His only clue to the channel was the color of the water and, sometimes, the speed of it. His sonar worked for a short while and then he shut it off. It kept bouncing back erratic signals from the bottom just beneath their keel. He watched as the *Urchin* nosed her way through swarms of water beetles that covered the surface of a spot near a bend like a moving, squirming mass of paint. On shore, the brilliant flash of a gold and blue macaw cut the endless green of the heavy vegetation. They passed two more small native villages, hardly more than a cluster of huts crowding the bank of the river. "Damn," Logan swore aloud as he wiped the perspiration from his chest only to have it trickle down his back. His hands on the wheel were wet from the intense concentration of guiding the *Urchin* through the shallow spots, the tricky currents at the turns of the river. A large island loomed up in midriver, about the size of a football field in length and about half as wide. Logan steered to the right of it and felt the sound of the *Urchin's* propellers tipping the mud, stirring up the murky water. He gunned the engines and the boat shot forward and he held her close as he dared to the shore, keeping away from the edge of the island. The islands, he noted, were nothing much more than small collections of trees on a base of earth rising up like so many humps on the back of an endless caterpillar. Golden marmosets and squirrel monkeys were scampering among the trees.

Except for the occasional small village they passed, there was only the unending lush green foliage of the banks. And yet he knew a thousand eyes were watching the *Urchin* as she slowly made her way upriver. Somewhere, someplace, there were hostile, prying eyes. He could feel it in his bones. For him and the *Urchin* this lush, burning land was a place of potential danger and that fact brought out the steel-wire hardness in him. Threats from outside always did. He had always made threats into a simple decision of win or lose and he didn't like losing, ever. There was danger here, he knew. It hung in the air like the heavy scent of the dense foliage and it made him think about Ariana and the unanswered questions about her. And then, with surprising suddenness, it was night. There was no slow sinking of the sun over the ocean water, no gradual disappearance over the horizon. There was heat, and then a grayness and dark, falling like a curtain. With the night came a chorus of new sounds from the thick foliage on both sides of the river. Logan dropped anchor quickly, felt it catch into sand and finally hold. Below decks, Ariana had turned on the cabin light and had dinner ready. Once more, he saw the little-girl enthusiasm of her, the eager wanting to please. It was nice to be near her again, he admitted to himself. He'd almost forgotten what it was like. The tiredness in him started to fade. The tension only retreated a little. He was pouring himself a jigger of warm Tennessee "sippin' whiskey" when Ariana came back into the cabin. Her fingers were smooth on the back of his neck. He reached up to pull her down on his lap when he saw her eyes widen as she looked past his shoulder. He cut off her scream with his hand and whirled.

"A face," she gasped, tearing his hand away. "At the porthole window. I saw it."

"Dammit!" Logan swore and raced up the companionway just in time to hear the sounds of someone swimming frantically away. He switched on the *Urchin's* searchlight beam over the top of the pilot house. He swept the water and halted, holding the fight on a man swimming furiously for shore. Ariana was beside him.

"Keep the light on him," he growled. "Don't lose him."

He didn't dare risk a dive in these shallow waters. He dropped over the side and went after the swimmer. The big Colt Python was still in his belt but he didn't want to use it. Shooting would only bring others and trouble. The man lost time by trying to dodge from the beam of the searchlight but Ariana kept it on him. Logan clambered ashore only seconds after him and saw him disappear into the thickness of the brush and the trees. Moving at a crouch, Logan followed and once inside the tangled foliage, he stopped and listened. There was silence and he rose on the balls of his feet, ready to move fast in any direction. The man was near, staying still. Logan moved, slowly, now, his eyes trying to make out shapes in the blackness of the forest. He moved behind the thick trunk of a tree, leaned against it and waited. Slowly, he bent down and felt along the base of the tree with his hands. He came up with three small twigs and a rock. One by one, he tossed them to the left, into the denseness. They landed with small, cracking sounds, as though someone was carefully moving off in that direction. In but a few moments, he heard the man start to move away and, stepping from behind the tree, he saw the black bulk of his figure. Logan moved with the speed of a panther pouncing, stealth disregarded for swiftness. The man whirled and Logan glimpsed a young face, brown-skinned with long black hair, one of the Indian natives of the region, and then he was on him, carrying him backward to the ground. Logan smashed a short, chopping right to the man's jaw as he landed on top of him. His knee sunk deep into the man's abdomen and he felt his quarry's legs draw up in pain. But the man managed to get an arm up and Logan saw the dull glint of steel. He grabbed the wrist as the knife started to come down and pressed the arm backward while his own elbow slammed into the man's throat. The arm went limp for an instant as the man gasped in pain, the knife falling to the ground. Logan had it in hand and slashed once with it, backward across the man's throat. There was a shuddered gasp and the lean, hard-eyed man sprang to his feet. He dropped the knife on the lifeless form and quickly moved out of the forest. Ariana, he saw as he hit the water, had had sense enough to douse the light. He swam quickly with long, powerful strokes and covered the short distance to the *Urchin* in seconds. The girl tossed him a line and he clambered aboard.

"He won't tell anyone he saw you," Logan said flatly. Ariana's eyes were round, troubled as she studied his face.

"What if he were just looking in?" she asked. "The people in these regions are very curious."

"A local Peeping Tom?" Logan snorted. "Then his career is over."

"Didn't you ask him, or try to find out?" she said.

"Why? I wouldn't have believed him anyway," Logan answered. "So trying to find out would only be something to help your conscience and I haven't got time for that crap."

"No time or no conscience?" she flared at him.

"You pick whichever you like," he said, his eyes hard.

"Logan," she said, her voice softening, "I'm sorry. I guess we're both a little on edge since starting upriver."

"I guess so," he said, his voice cold, flat. "I know I'm tired. I'm going to turn in."

He left her there and went to his cabin, pausing only to shower off the river water before climbing into the bunk. As he lay there, waiting for sleep, feeling the tense fatigue of his body, he thought of the girl's words about his lack of time or conscience and his eyes burned with a terrible coldness. Once he had indulged in both and paid a price beyond all the wealth in the world. He would never do it again. He turned over and went to sleep with never another thought of the lifeless form in the forest.

The day dawned hot and humid and as Logan rose, he looked out the porthole of the cabin to see a gray blanket of mist still over the river. He put on only trousers, tucking the big Colt Python into his belt again, and went to the aft cabin to wake the girl. She lay with a sheet half over her, breasts exposed, hair a black halo on the pillow. He went into the cabin and touched her breast, running his hand over its soft firmness and then put his fingers upon her cheek. He had only come to waken her but as she stirred, opened her eyes slid her arms around his neck, he put his lips to the delicate pink of her left breast. Her legs raised and moved languorously, like long stalks waving in a slow wind, and he went to her, moving his body onto hers, and once again she became his.

The sun had ripped the gray blanket of mist from the river when he finally slid from the bed to stand beside it.

"What a way to wake up," Ariana purred, stretching her long, lithe body. Logan went to the pilot house, angered in a way at himself. Not that he hadn't enjoyed, or wanted her. He just had decided it might be better without it now. There were still too many unanswered things about her role in this, too many small uncertainties that kept bothering him. And yet, she was so guileless sometimes, so little-girl in her openness. He opened the *Urchin's* engines as soon as the anchor came up and headed into midriver, still wondering about the girl. She popped up in the open hatch, handing him coffee, wearing only the pink shorts, looking like she had stepped to his boat from the marbled palace of a Roman emperor.

"You make it hard to concentrate on this damned river," he growled. She laughed, a very female little laugh.

"I'll put something on," she said. "The faster we get there, the sooner we can start back and that's what I really want."

It was not an unpleasant thought and Logan felt the small stirrings of anticipation inside himself. A week with Ariana would be something else, he knew. Now, their lovemaking had an unhappy aftertaste, at least to him, as though he had made love to a girl who was essentially a stranger. He corrected himself. Essentially a fraud. She was two or three people, separate and compartmented—a warm, enthusiastic girl who liked playing house and a wild, abandoned hedonist in bed. As he was thinking of her, she poked her head up through the hatchway with a map in her hand, no doubt extracted from the small canvas bag she'd brought aboard with her.

"We ought to be coming to two islands almost touching each other," she said. "That means we're making good time."

"I see them up ahead," Logan said. "Let's have a look at that map."

"Quechayo doesn't appear on it," she said, handing it to him. "But it'll be on our left and we ought to reach it by tomorrow night."

Logan looked at the map quickly. She was right, the village of Quechayo was unmarked. He gave the map back to her and started to edge the *Urchin* to starboard to skirt the two islands which lay almost end to end. Reaching the village tomorrow night was more than fine with him. He'd had enough of this damned river. Even now the sweat was coating his body as he played Russian roulette with sandbars, underwater roots and uncertain depths. Getting by the two islands took slow, careful going. The Tinina River was made for flatboats and rafts. They rounded a sharp bend and he saw a small native village, the first they'd passed in a good while, grass- and leaf-roofed huts, small, brownskinned naked children and women with loose, bright garments. The village disappeared from sight as they went on and only the walls of the unending green looked out at them. He wanted to watch the brilliant slashes of color that were the parrots and toucans, but always the river demanded his attention as the narrow channel meandered from side to side, first near one bank, then the other. He was glad to see the grayness descend which heralded night and he edged out of the channel and dropped anchor. Ariana came on deck as the blackness closed around them, sandwiches on a tray. He ate and stretched out on a deck chair. The clicking, clacking, chirping and buzzing of a thousand different kinds of insects filled the thick air, echoing across the river from bank to bank. He went below, fixed two stiff bourbons and brought them back on deck.

"A nightcap," he said. "I'm finishing this and going to sleep. The earlier we get started in the morning the happier I'll be."

The bourbon was good going down and it even gave him a lift to stay on deck longer. But he fought it down and went below. He stripped to his shorts and lay down on the bunk, stretching out on his stomach. He heard Ariana's footsteps and started to get up on one elbow but she was in the cabin and beside the bunk in an instant, her hands massaging his back, rubbing, kneading, working out the tensions of his neck and shoulder muscles.

"Mmmmm, nice," he murmured. Her fingers, which could stroke and caress, could also press with surprising strength, he found.

"When we get back, you and the *Urchin* are coming with me," she said. "I'll show you a new world, Logan, a world you'll like."

"I have a world and I like it," he murmured.

"You'll like mine better," she said. He didn't answer. He just fell asleep under the relaxing touch of her hands.

He was alone when he woke and he didn't know how long he'd slept. He just suddenly awoke, his subconscious alarm ringing loudly inside his head. It wasn't the feel of danger so much as the feel of something gone, something missing. He went out onto the deck softly, on cat feet, moving like a panther on the prowl. He saw the pink shorts and the white halter top lying on the deck and he crouched down beside the rail, his eyes scanning the water, trying to pierce the darkness. Suddenly, on the nearest bank, he saw a light blink on and off. He watched and his eyes made out the figure on the shore, ghost-white. He went to the pilot house, got his field glasses and returned to the rail. Through the glasses he could see, not well, but better. Ariana was on the bank, in bra and bikini panties, and she was blinking the light on and off again. She did it every half minute or so, flashing to the opposite shore. Logan watched in silence and then he heard the soft sound of water being disturbed. He swung the glasses to the opposite shore and saw the dark figure of a man poling a small raft into the river. Ariana's flashing light went out and Logan watched the man move toward her, poling the raft against the slow current. As he reached the shore, Ariana moved toward him and stretched out a hand. The man handed her something and immediately started to pole away downriver. Logan saw the girl wait for a moment, watching him go, and then walk into the water and strike out for the boat. Field glasses resting on the top of the rail, he watched her approach, saw her white arms rising and falling in the darkness as she swam toward him. He stayed as long as he dared and saw that in one hand she held something rolled up, scroll-like. Grim-lipped, he retreated to his cabin and lay back on the bunk, face-down. He heard her climb aboard, pause at the door of his cabin, and then go on. She's doing a good job, he admitted to himself, silent, smooth, efficient. He lay still and let an hour go by before he rose. This time, it was his tall figure that moved silently and paused at a cabin door, listening to the sounds of her even, steady breathing. He went into the cabin and his eyes immediately found the small, canvas bag on the ledge beside the bed. He reached inside it, felt a hairbrush, a rolled-up blouse, comb, extra sandals and then the small, wet, rolled object. He pulled it out and went up on deck. In the pilot house, he turned on the soft green of the instrument lights and unrolled the object. It was a photostat, plasticized to make it waterproof. He felt the frown creasing his brow as he looked at it. It was a dental chart and in the upper right-hand corner was the name of one Charles Panico. Logan found himself whistling silently as he studied the chart. It was an ordinary enough dental chart, except that five of the teeth were marked with an X, two lateral incisors, two anterior molars and one upper canine. The X, of course, could mean anything. It could mean simply that those teeth had fillings, or needed work or any number of things. But then, it could also have a special meaning. It was a special chart, special in importance, it seemed, and he asked himself what the hell did she need with a dead man's dental chart? He rolled the chart up again, tiptoed back into the cabin with the sleeping girl and put it back into the little canvas bag. Then he went on deck to think, starting at the beginning. This is almost like old times, he told himself grimly.

First, the man Alvarez had lied to him. He had known that when Alvarez had caught himself at mention of the name Camacho. Then there was Ariana, the girl of obvious breeding and background who didn't fit into this kind of role. Yet she was here and ready with evasions and deft turn-away answers to any probing about Panico. Logan's eyes were narrowed and he felt the icy coldness stirring inside him. He didn't like being lied to or played for a fool. And Ariana was holding to her role, keeping it separate from what she felt for him. He knew she had come to want him for more than a toy. It was in her eyes, it was in the flaring anger that came out when she thought of her job. She was feeling the inner turmoil, the pain, of keeping separate accounts. But whether she wanted to or not, she was lying to him, and her games were more intricate than he'd suspected, which brought him back to the dental chart. It was plain that it had been arranged that she be given the dental chart only when they neared their objective. She obviously wasn't to risk carrying it around, in case something went wrong. That made it a rather special dental chart. His mind raced on. Dental charts were often used for identification purposes. Nothing wrong there. But then anyone could have taken it and done this job. Ariana was here because she was one of the few people able to identify Panico the guerrilla leader on sight. That's what they'd told him, anyway, and it brought back the question of questions. Why, if she knew him would she need a dental chart in her hot little hands? And what of the X-marked teeth? Did they mean anything special?

Nothing really fitted, he realized. He had only questions and no answers. All he knew about Panico was what he'd been told. He did know one thing. He was mad as hell and getting madder. He'd been beaten and shot at, blackmailed into being here, been lied to by a smooth operator and now by a beautiful girl, a girl who was, herself, still a big question mark. Inside that gorgeous wrapping there existed hard-steel determination. Only because of it could that kind of girl come from her background into this kind of task. Only because of it could that kind of girl make love the way she did. But, Logan promised himself, he'd get at the truth before too much time went by. He decided to say nothing about what he'd seen. Maybe she'd open up to him before they reached Quechayo. He closed his eyes and dropped off to sleep.

The smell of scrambled eggs woke him and he slipped on his trousers in the gray dawn light, pushing the Colt Python into his belt. Ariana came in with a tray and plates of eggs and toast.

"How is our supply holding out?" he asked.

"Fine," she said. "You've a big freezer on this boat."

"Specially built for me," he commented. Ariana seemed happy and chattery with uncontained excitement. "Mostly I'm thinking about going back home with you," she said, and he wished he didn't doubt her. She obviously expected everything would go smoothly.

"I'll show you an inlet, Logan," Ariana said, her eyes taking on a soft, dreamy quality, "where the sea comes in through a narrow rocky bridge and the house goes down to the water. It's your own ocean pool, clear and cool and calm even on rough days."

"Your place?" he asked casually.

"Maybe someday," she answered. He waited till she had put the plates on the tray and picked up the tray to go to the galley. "Who's Camacho?" he asked mildly.

He saw the moment's pause, the twitch of her jaw and the way her hand tightened on the tray. He smiled, inwardly, with admiration, at how quickly she recovered and looked at him with round, big eyes.

"Camacho?" she repeated. "Where'd you get that name?"

"Heard it around," he answered.

"I haven't," she said. She went on into the galley and Logan's smile was thin as he pulled up anchor and kicked over the engines. He found that the Tinina had narrowed still farther and each island left less room to skirt around it.

"How are we doing?" Ariana asked, popping her head through the hatch near midday.

"You could swim upriver faster than we're going."

"Not this far inland," she said, a grimness in her voice that made him look at her. "Piranhas," she explained. "Up here the river is full of them. Nobody swims here for very long."

Logan's eyes automatically scanned the water. The piranha moved in schools, he knew, and were probably the most vicious of all underwater river life. He had once seen them strip a cow to bare bones in less then five minutes, and that was something you didn't forget.

"Okay, no swimming," he said. They were skirting a small island that turned out to be wider than he'd realized. Suddenly he heard the *Urchin's* keel dig in deeply, her headway grind to a halt and he quickly switched off the engines. Ariana's head popped up.

"We're hung up," he said angrily. "We really dug in this time. I don't know if it's sand or mud. More important, I don't know if the screws are in it. I've got to go down and take a look. It's not deep, that much we know."

He read the question in her eyes. It wasn't deep but the piranhas weren't concerned about that, either. He took out his keys and opened a tall, thin locker in the side of the pilot house. Six highly polished rifles gleamed in it, each in their own stand. Taking a Browning Double Automatic shotgun, he handed it to Ariana.

"You'll have to go on deck. Try and stay behind the rail," he said. "You'll be able to see them coming, if they come. Fire a blast into them. The rest will be kept busy chewing up their schoolmates for a while."

He went on deck, stripped to his shorts and lowered himself over the side. Submerged, he struck out for the stem of the vessel and saw that things were not as bad as he'd feared. A high ridge cut across the channel and the *Urchin* had cut into it all the way to the start of the aft cabin. But her screws were free and the ridge was sand, not mud. He knew what had to be done and it wouldn't be difficult. Just to make certain, he surfaced and swam around to the shore side of the boat, in case there was anything he'd missed on the other side. Ariana had crossed the deck to keep watch on him and as he surfaced he heard her short cry of terror.

"Behind you!" she gasped. He whirled just as the snake struck and he felt the fangs sink into his thigh. He saw the snake's head, lance-shaped, and the blue-gray marks on its hide as it swam quickly away, pointed like the tip of an arrowhead, and he knew he was in trouble. Ariana had tossed him a line and he grabbed it and pulled himself up. Her eyes, full of fear, told him his guess was right.

"Goddamn," he cursed and started for the cabin. "There's a snake-bite kit in the bathroom cabinet and serum in the refrigerator." She didn't have to be told to move fast and Logan felt the numbness in his thigh as he stretched out on the bunk. Damn my stinking luck, he swore silently. Though not a water snake, the fer-de-lance took to the water occasionally. Logan had had to be around on one of those occasions. The fer-de-lance was deadlier than the rattler, its poison swifter. He watched as Ariana ran back into the cabin with the serum in the hypodermic. She injected it quickly, making a face of her own as she did so. Then she made a tourniquet, put a suction cup on the small wound and began to suck out the blood. He let her, saying nothing. His life depended on two things, neither of which he nor anyone else could do a damn about. One was the serum. It either took, proved potent enough, or it didn't. The other was the possibility that being in the water had immediately washed out some of the venom. If that had happened, he might make it. Otherwise, the world population would go down by one. The water and the serum, one or the other or both. He closed his eyes. His leg was beginning to hurt.

The girl made two small razor-blade cuts in his leg and moved the tourniquet up and put the suction cup on the incisions. There is no need to worry about anchoring, Logan told himself. They were wedged into the sandbar and very secure. He lay still. The less movement the better. Ariana stood beside him, looking down at him.

"Maybe I can get help," she said. "I'll try to find a village."

He managed a grin. "Maybe something from a local witch doctor," he said.

"I can't just stand here," Ariana exploded.

"You can sit down," he said. "And that's about all you can do, now. The serum bottle says I can get another dose in eight hours. If I'm around to take it, that is. Don't worry. I'm not easy to kill."

His head was suddenly feeling very light and the cabin was doing funny things, moving around, getting smaller and larger and then smaller again. He closed his eyes. It didn't make much difference. He got a sharp stabbing pain in the abdomen and his legs drew up involuntarily. Drawing a deep breath, he relaxed his body and stretched out again. He wanted a drink of good bourbon but he was still conscious enough to know better. He snapped his eyes open with a determined effort and saw Ariana at the side of the bunk. She had brought a high stool over and was perched on it. Again he managed a reassuring smile. He hadn't been exactly kidding her. He was a hard man to kill. He was a hard man to do anything with. But it was that very hardness that would help him now, he knew. It took over and fought for him as his body began to pour perspiration and his breath grow shallow and labored. For a while he could hear himself breathing hard and then he lost contact with himself. A strange darkness settled over him that was neither death nor life but some nether world suspended in between. It was a funny world made up of shadows and names without voices, faces without bodies. He heard himself talking, calling out, but it was as if he were inside some giant bottle and everyone else was outside staring in at him. He saw faces from the past pressed against the glass, there for a moment and then vanishing before his eyes. He saw Willie the Beaver and Henny D'Angelo. He saw the big sign that said *Private* and he saw feet chasing, running, and guns that fired soundlessly. And then the faces and names all faded away and he heard himself calling out again, calling into emptiness.

Is that me shaking? he wondered. Is that my body that feels so cold? How could he be hot and cold all at once? Then suddenly, or it seemed suddenly, he was burning up, his body afire, his throat aflame and he lay still while the fire consumed him. It went on consuming him, and on and on until finally there was nothing and he was falling, falling. Darkness had been his, and now it wrapped itself even tighter around him, squeezing him into nothingness. Silence, utter silence, his mind turned off and he lay still.

It was far into the night, turning toward dawn, when the tall, lean man stirred and his eyes fluttered, then opened. The girl sitting curled up on the bunk opposite him was asleep, no more than a blurred outline at first. It was perhaps a half hour before his eyes could focus enough to see her as a person. He tried to lift his head but it wouldn't lift. He felt as though he had been turned inside out, was drained of every drop of blood, the limpest of limp rags. But as his eyes took in the cabin, every corner familiar to him, he smiled and there was a line of triumph in the smile. He was alive and now, consciously, he put together again what had happened. It had been the snake, of course, the goddamned snake in the water. Ariana had given him the serum and it had worked. Probably the venom had partially washed out in the water, too. Whatever had done it, he was alive and all the things that still waited to be done still lay ahead. But not now, not till morning. He managed to turn his head and go to sleep.

He woke first, in the morning, and saw Ariana in the bunk across from him, still asleep where she'd curled up. He felt less limp. As he struggled up on one elbow, he realized that he was in something less than championship shape. The noise of his movement woke the girl and she jumped from the bed and was at his side, her arms cradling his head against the white halter top, her breasts pressed into his face. He had to admit it was a nice way to be greeted.

"Oh, God, you're alive," she said, looking down at him. "I didn't think you'd make it."

"I told you I'm hard to kill," he grinned, sitting up and letting the dizziness go away.

"Did I put cold compresses on you!" she said. "All night, one after another." He let his eyes search hers. The relief he saw there was genuine enough. But all the deceits and lies and unanswered questions flooded back into his mind and he knew that nothing had really changed. He was alive and they were still heading for the village of Quechayo and she was still playing it her way. And he was going to get at the truth his way.

"I'll make tea," Ariana said. "It's what you need this morning."

Logan waited till she went to the galley, then he slid from the bunk and tried his legs. They, wavered a while, then straightened out. He stretched them, moved, put on trousers, and began to feel alive. Ariana returned with the tea and it felt good, invigorating.

"You were delirious, you know," she said casually.

"I didn't know," he commented dryly.

"And you talked a lot."

He felt his jaw set and an invisible mask descend over his face.

"Were you ever a private investigator, Logan?" she asked. He chose his spare, terse answers carefully and let the smile stay on his face.

"I sounded like that?" he said.

"Yes."

"As you said, I was delirious. God knows what I said. It could have been anything."

She was looking at him out of the corner of her eyes, studying his impassive face, the smile that masked rather then revealed.

"Who was Nancy?" she asked casually.

It was hard keeping the smile but he managed it.

"Did I talk about a Nancy?" he asked.

"Not exactly talk," the girl said. "More like calling. In fact you called for a Nancy one and a Nancy two. Very confusing, I must say."

He shrugged. "To me, too," he said.

"You're lying, Logan," she said flatly.

"I'm just not remembering," he said. He got up. "I'm going to get us off this sandbar."

"You're not well enough," she said, quickly. "You need more rest."

"I'm all right," he said, almost angrily. He didn't tell her that her questions had sent cold determination and anger and pain through him like a shot of adrenalin. He had remembered, all right, with a memory that seared and burned. It was funny-sad how it always happened at the dark times, the times when he needed help. Her face or her name, it was always there. He climbed onto the seat before the wheel, switched on the engines, let them run for a moment and then put them into reverse at full throttle. The *Urchin* shuddered only a moment, then pulled back out of the sandbar. He reversed engines immediately, before he backed into some other ridge hidden in the murky water. He sent the boat forward at full speed, feeling her bite into the shallow water, protesting that there wasn't enough for her to grab. But she hit the sandbar and went right on through, spewing sand up into the water as the twin screws churned through it, and they were in free water again. He slowed down and proceeded at the deliberate pace they'd used all along. Ariana stayed below once again and he heard her pacing the cabin. The closer they came to Quechayo, the more she paced, and Logan's grin grew grimmer. She refused to level with him. Her plans, whatever they were, stayed set, and so would his.

But progress was slow in the narrowness of the river. He saw four schools of piranha. He knew there were a lot more that he hadn't seen. It was still light but a gray hint of night was coloring the sky when they came into sight of the village, on their left, where she said it would be.

"Quechayo," he called to her and knew she'd be glued to a porthole. As they drew abreast of the village he saw four wharves jutting out from the bank and then the wooden houses amid the thatched leaf huts stretching back from the shoreline. Quechayo was larger than it appeared from the river bank. He glimpsed a half-dozen men wearing cartridge belts slung over their shoulders, carbines in their hands, watching him move by. Children waved and he waved back. He was past the village in a minute and he continued on, maintaining the slow, steady speed. About three-quarters of a mile ahead he saw another small island. It would be perfect for his plans. It was dark when he nosed around it and dropped anchor in midriver, off the far tip of the island. He moved around the *Urchin* in the dark, gathering bits and pieces of equipment from fore and aft. From the aft locker, he pulled out a small rubber raft and inflated it on the deck. Ariana had come out and offered to help. He cheerfully let her finish inflating it. While she was doing that, he took some canned food, a tin of biscuits and filled a plastic bottle with fresh water. He put all that into a plastic bag.

"What on earth is all that for?" Ariana asked, a small furrow creasing her smooth forehead.

"It's a CARE package," he said, cheerfully, and watched her frown deepen. He lowered the raft into the water and tossed a piece of dried meat he'd taken from the freezer into the river. The water boiled furiously for a minute and then subsided.

"The river is sure filled with them," he said to Ariana, and watched her shudder.

"I still don't understand what your 'CARE package' is for," she said.

"I might run into trouble in Quechayo," he said. "One never knows. I might have to lay low for a whole day. Meantime, you might get hungry on that island."

He saw her frown really deepen and her eyes darken.

"Just what do you mean by that?" she asked, her voice ominous.

"I mean that you've been lying to me from the start, you and Alvarez," Logan said. "Now I'm going to find out a few things for myself while you stay on that island. I know you won't be swimming off and I don't want you to get hungry."

"You'll do no such thing," she said, flaring. "And I haven't lied to you."

"That a girl, keep pitching," Logan said. "But you're going on that island unless you start leveling with me. Let's try the dental chart for openers.

He saw her eyes widen in surprise and his grin was cold. "Still want to play games?" he asked.

"Logan," she began, moving toward him, her eyes wide and deep. "Trust me. Please. I can't tell you more than that. Not now, anyway." Her hands were against his chest, her eyes imploring.

She could be meaning every word, he knew. Or she could be a damned good little actress. It was natural to most women, anyway. But she'd forgotten that man at the porthole. He didn't take chances, not anymore.

"Sorry, doll," he said, his voice hard, unyielding. "I'm very poor at trusting, especially when I've been played along. The game is over. Talk or I take it alone."

The girl was going to try to reach the tall, stone-faced man again but the expression in his eyes told her it would be a waste of time. She stepped back, paused, and then made a flying dive for the bunk, reaching her hand under the mattress. But Logan had her wrist as her fingers closed over the snub-nosed Smith and Wesson .38 Police special. She had had the gun when she had come aboard and shot out the lights of the patrol boat, but he'd quite forgotten about it. She clawed at him with her other hand and he spun her around, turned her wrist backward and pressed. She cried out in pain and the gun fell from her grip. He caught it, spun her around and slammed her into the wall. She aimed a kick at his groin and he half-turned to take it on the leg. Eyes blazing fury, her voice half-sobbing in anger, she tried to duck under his arm. He brought a short, chopping right up that caught the very point of her lovely chin and she went down in a heap, rag doll fashion. He lifted her over his shoulder, took the plastic bag of food and went on deck. He lowered her into the raft and paddled to the island. She was still out as he dumped her on the sand and put the: bag of food beside her. He returned to the *Urchin*, got a large burlap bag from a closet, and took another look at the dental chart before he heard her call. Burlap sack in hand, the big Colt Python in his belt, he swung down onto the raft.

"Damn you, Logan," he heard Ariana call. "You don't know what you're doing. Take me with you." She could see him moving past on the little raft, paddling silently. He waved an arm to her and went on. She was right, of course. He wouldn't know if the body was really the guerrilla leader's or not. He'd find out when he returned with it to the boat. He took the raft downriver, almost to the very edge of the village of Quechayo, before he paddled into shore and pulled it up into the thick foliage. He didn't want to have to lug his grisly burden far. He'd never dug up a grave before. Hell, he wasn't even a member of the Gravediggers' Union.

CHAPTER EIGHT

The village of Quechayo, as he'd glimpsed when he and the *Urchin* passed by it, ran far deeper than it appeared to go. Making his way along the edge, he saw a number of well-built wooden houses and one clay structure surrounded by a cluster of smaller ones. The cemetery was the last thing in the village, almost outside it at the very far end and, when he reached it, he realized that neither he nor the girl had thought of the one thing needed for gravedigging, a shovel. But he was glad to see that the cemetery was a fairly large one with a tool shack to the side. He crept to the shack, found a shovel, and began to move silently among the small mounds. All had some sort of headstone or marking, in many cases merely a stick of wood with a name cut into it. Off to the right, at the very edge of the cemetery, he found the one he thought he wanted, marked with a wooden post and the initial *P.* dug into it. He was surprised that it was marked it at all. He pushed the shovel into the ground and tossed aside a clump of earth. The ground was soft and he could dig silently. Soon he had a sizable amount dug up and he saw the one end of a plain, pine box. He paused to wipe the perspiration from his hands and face. He wanted to get the hell away from this damn spot. The whole thing was giving him a very funny feeling. Dammit, he told himself angrily. Stop being a kid on Halloween and get on with it.

He got on with it but the feeling wouldn't go away. Good, small-town upbringing never really shook itself loose. The Golden

Rule, church every Sunday, honor thy father and mother, respect for the dead and all the rest of the traditional virtues. He'd shot holes in most of them long ago and this made one more. The pine box was uncovered, now, and he put down the shovel. On his hands and knees, he reached down and lifted the cover of the crude casket. The corpse lay there, naked, looking more like some waxen figure than anything else. Logan saw the three small bullet holes in the chest, the discolored tissues surrounding each hole. He had expected more stench, and there was the smell of death, but it wasn't as bad as he'd feared. Formaldehyde had apparently been used in massive doses on the body and the interior of the pine casket and it had so far succeeded in keeping the hordes of creeping, crawling creatures to a minimum. Logan let his eyes rove over the body. Panico had been fairly tall but slender, his face thin and drawn, more so now, of course. The skin had started to pull together, making the body seem older then it actually was. He surveyed his prize, distastefully but with some satisfaction. He'd learned a little. There was a body buried under the marking *P*. And it had three bullet holes in it. That much tied in with the story of the guerrilla leader's possible death during the battle with the government forces. But was this really Panico? He'd hoped the man would have been clothed, with something on him to provide a clue. He decided he'd have a look at those teeth. He remembered which had been marked with the *X* on the chart. Maybe he'd find out that all the marks meant were that the teeth were missing.

He spread the burlap sack out and lay flat on the ground to reach down into the coffin. He got his hand onto an arm, cold, wax fruit, a brittle feel as though a little too much pressure would tear away the skin. He lifted, slowly, and the body started to rise, stiffly, and then with a dry, cracking sound, bent in two. Logan kept his mouth tightly closed. The body rose further. He had it almost sitting up when the voice cut through the night, a deep, clear voice.

"That will be enough, *amigo,*" the voice said. "Put him back."

Logan didn't look up but just opened his hand and let the body slide from his grasp. It fell back into the coffin with a small thump.

"Now we will have a little talk, whoever you are," the voice said. Logan's eyes cast around and he saw boots, at least six pairs, with more coming to stand on the other side of the grave. He raised himself just enough to look behind him and see the big man standing there, a heavy, jowled face with a big nose and a drooping mustache under a white, floppy hat. The man wore a cartridge belt slung across his chest and two guns in a gunbelt. Behind him, in ragged, tattered clothes, three men waited, two with carbines. Logan turned his head to see the three standing on the other side of the open grave. Just past them was the forest.

"On your feet, *pronto!*" the big man with the floppy white hat commanded, impatience suddenly in his voice. Logan drew up one knee as if he were starting to rise and then, with one motion, he had the Colt Python in his hand and was firing in a sweeping arc. He didn't aim, he just let go a blast of lead in all directions. The big man and the others dived away as the heavy Colt slugs tore through the air. He heard two voices cry out in pain as he leaped forward, across the open grave, and streaked for the woods.

"*¡VIVO!*" he heard the big man yell. *Alive!* They didn't want him dead, not yet, anyway. He crashed into the thickness of the forest only to find it was filled with a reception committee. They had been there, in hiding, he realized at once, watching the gravesight. Two men tried a tackle and he kicked the first one in the face and heard him scream. The second one got his leg and Logan brought the heavy butt of the Colt down on the back of his head. The man dropped off like a fly. There was still a shot in the Colt and he fired pointblank at a wild-eyed character leaping at him. The figure spun in midair, kicking his legs out in a last protest against death, and fell at his feet. He whirled, swinging the butt end of the Colt in a wide arc as he heard others crashing up behind him. He saw the gun split the face of one man, sending a geyser of blood spurting from it and his attacker dropped to his knees, both hands clutched at his face. Logan kicked him hard and he went over backward. Logan ducked the vicious swing of a carbine and felt it graze his hair. He sunk his arm almost to the elbow into the riflewielding man's stomach and the figure doubled over. Logan grabbed the carbine just as someone slammed into him with a flying tackle, catching him around the middle. He brought the rifle down on the back of the man's neck but another figure leaped on his back He fell forward, twisting so that he landed atop the man on his back. He saw the butt of a rifle descending on him and he turned his head. The blow landed too high on his head and though he felt the sharp pain of it he was very much conscious. He grabbed at the legs nearest and yanked. Their owner fell in a tangled heap and Logan pulled free of the man under him. He came up swinging, felt his fists strike flesh and blood, felt figures giving way, falling, and then the blow hit hard against his temple, the stock of a carbine swung flat. He fell sideways to his knees. A kick sent him sprawling to the ground. He tried rolling over to catapult to his feet but they were on him, rifle butts and feet slamming into him. The lights began to go out. He shook his head, tried to grab at something, anything, and then blackness swept over him and he felt himself falling as if through a deep tunnel.

When he woke it was with light seeping through his fluttering eyelids, bright light, and the shapes swimming in front of him slowly took form. The first form was the big man, still wearing the floppy white hat. His drooping mustache materialized first and then the rest of his face, like an out-of-focus movie screen being brought into focus. Logan looked around. He was in a room with unpainted clay walls, some wooden chairs and a table. The big man was watching him and two others with rifles stood by the door. Logan saw that his hands were tied in front of him and he was lying in a corner of the room. At a signal from the big man, one of the guards came over and lifted Logan onto a chair. Head cleared, Logan's eyes narrowed as he noted the small window of the room, the one door. It opened as he looked at it and a girl came with black hair came into the room. She wore a low-necked peasant blouse and a green wool skirt. Large, heavy breasts swung pendulously as she leaned against the big man.

"That's him?" she asked, gesturing toward Logan, contempt in her eyes. "He does not look like so much."

"That's because you are a woman and a poor judge of fighting men," the man answered. "He has the body of a jaguar. And the disposition, too, I think."

Logan let a thin smile cross his face. The big man's eyes were serious.

"Who are you?" he said, suddenly. "How did they get you into this?"

"I was hired," Logan said. "The name is Logan."

"You are the fourth one to try to get to Panico," the big man said. "You are the only one to get through to the cemetery. Later you must tell me how you managed to get by our sentries. Unfortunately, the others were all shot and killed before we could question them. But you are alive."

He smiled, a not unpleasant smile. Only the glitter of his dark eyes revealed its real meaning. "If you want to stay alive, you will answer my questions," he said. "It is lucky we had men posted at the grave, watching from the trees, no?" He had turned to the woman and she nodded, her eyes still on Logan.

"I still cannot understand how he did so much damage," she muttered. "Jorge dead. Aquito dead. Morales, too. Poor Costallacho so badly hurt he cannot see to walk. Quinachi, too."

"Believe me, he did it," the man said. "But if we can get the truth from him it will have been worth it." He turned to Logan and his voice dropped a few notches as he spoke.

"You say you were hired," he began. "Who hired you?"

"A man named Alvarez," Logan answered.

"To bring back Panico's body, yes?"

Logan nodded. It was as good a story as any he could come up with at the moment.

"Why is Panico so valuable to them?" the big man shot out, quickly, pounding his fist into his palm. "Why must they have him?"

Logan studied the intensity in the man's eyes. It was an odd question, he thought. This big man had obviously taken over upon the death of the guerrilla leader.

"You ought to know the answer to that one," Logan said. The big man's eyes flickered for a moment.

"You tell me the answer," he said. "Maybe I am stupid." This man might be a lot of things but stupid wasn't one of them, Logan was convinced. His eyes were too bright, too quick, too canny. But he felt his own temper rising. What the hell kind of a cat and mouse game were they playing with him?

"They want him for the same reason you buried him here in this stinking little hole and put a guard around his grave," Logan said.

"We buried him here and put the guard out because we realized he was so valuable to Alvarez and his group," the man said.

"You're full of shit," Logan answered, his temper flaring. "You don't want it known that your great guerrilla leader, the spirit of your crummy revolution, is dead. No big leader, no big revolution."

"Ay!" it was the girl's voice. "He is *loco*, this one. Maybe he fights good but he is *loco*."

The big man held out a hand and she fell silent at once. "Wait a minute," he said. "Say that again, *amigo*. We have buried our dead leader, yes? And we don't want the people to know he is dead, eh?"

"That's right," Logan said, and suddenly he had a very funny feeling. The man seemed to be leading him along and suddenly he wasn't sure where the road was going.

"And our dead leader's name? Come, come, *amigo*. His name?"

"Maybe you are stupid," Logan said. "Panico."

He saw the big man shoot a glance at the girl, his lips open up in a soundless laugh. And then the sound followed, a deep-chested roaring laugh that started slowly and built up into a hurricane of bellowing. The girl has joined in and had buried her head in his wide chest. Logan watched with a strange uneasy feeling. Suddenly the big man stopped his roaring laughter and lashed out with one foot. His boot caught the front leg of the chair and, as he yanked, Logan went sprawling onto the floor. The boot lashed out again and he felt the sharp, stabbing pain as it landed in his ribs, rolling him over and into the wall. The big man was standing over him and Logan tried a kick of his own. He was in a poor position and the kick only grazed the man's kneecap.

"You know who is stupid, *amigo*?" Logan saw the drooping mustache quiver. "You are stupid, that is who."

He turned to the girl and the two guards, including them all in his bellow. "Who leads the movement?" he yelled.

"Camacho!" they said as one. "¡Viva Camacho!" The big man turned to Logan and pounded his chest with one huge fist.

"Me, Camacho," he roared. "I lead the people's movement. I lead the revolution."

A few things were snapping into place while an icy fury gathered inside Logan at the same time, things such as a figure in the cabin door yelling ¡Viva Camacho!, and Alvarez's pause at the name. Ariana, too.

"You are Camacho," Logan said, his voice flat. "And you lead the movement. Then who the hell is Panico?"

"One of Alvarez's men," Camacho said.

Camacho reached down, picked Logan up like a child and put him back on the chair. He was grinning broadly and Logan felt his temper rocket. He didn't like being taken. He didn't like being laughed at, either. A few things were falling into place, but only a few and not nearly enough.

"So that's what they told you, eh?" Camacho laughed again. "You were going to bring back the body of the big leader of the revolutionary movement so they could be sure he was dead."

"That's what they told me," Logan said flatly. Camacho laughed again and leaned into Logan's face.

"Tell me, do I look dead to you?" he roared, grinning.

"Not near dead enough."

"Watch your tongue," Camacho snarled. "I'm not sure I believe this crazy story of yours."

"Believe whatever you want," Logan said. "It happens to be the truth."

"And you do not know why this Panico is so valuable to Alvarez?" Camacho barked. Logan shook his head.

"I told you what they told me about him," he answered. *That* wasn't really a lie. He didn't know what made the corpse so damned important. He had a few new ideas, but he didn't really know.

"Take him away," Camacho suddenly barked at the guards. "I want to think about this a little bit more."

Logan was pulled to his feet and led outside. He saw he had been inside the largest of the clay structures he'd noted when he skirted the village. They led him to one of the smaller ones that half-encircled it, opened a door and threw him in. He landed on a dirt floor in a pitch-black room. Well, almost pitch-black, he noted, as a sliver of the outside night came in through an air hole about a foot long and three inches wide. His hands still bound in front of him, he crawled to one of the walls and sat down with his back to it. Alone in the dark, he tried to sort out what he had learned this far. The story he'd been given by Alvarez, and carried on by Ariana, had been simple, logical, easy to swallow. And he'd swallowed it, hook, line and sinker. He had had some misgivings and suspicions, finally, but he'd never really suspected the truth about Panico. And just what was the truth about the man? As Camacho had said, he was very important to Alvarez and his group. Logan wondered who the hell the group was if not the Peruvian Government. He wished he had the girl here and could wring some answers from her gorgeous lying little throat. But he brought his mind back to Panico. Alvarez and Ariana wanted to get to him and wanted it very badly, enough to hire him, make up a phony story and risk their own necks, or hers, anyway. Suddenly that dental chart began to make real sense. Panico was important, all right, and it had something to do with what was in his mouth. He was dead but he had plenty to say. Ariana had known that right along, of course. Her job had been to get at the body and those teeth. Identification was never even in the picture. If Alvarez had a group, what kind of a group was it? Were they in the Peruvian Government? Ariana was part of it, that was certain. Camacho's opinions couldn't be taken seriously, he knew. If they were really the Peruvian Government force, and had seen fit to tell him a story for their own reasons, Camacho would castigate them too. The man was a revolutionary, an antigovernment leader. Damn, Logan swore. He had to find a way out of this place. He could almost sympathize with Camacho's frustration. He was feeling pretty damned frustrated himself. They were all frustrated, Ariana, Camacho and himself, for different reasons. Camacho had a prize, a valuable corpse, and he didn't know why it was so damned valuable. Ariana had an island to herself and nothing more and he had a dark hole and the prospects of being killed before he ever really learned the truth. Damn, Logan muttered again. He started to crawl around the little cubicle in the dark, feeling with his hands for a sharp rock, a pointed stick, anything that might be used to cut the wrist ropes. But there was only loose soil on the ground and he got to his feet and ran his hands along the walls. The clay was rough but not rough enough. He scraped the ropes against one part, only to finally realize that all he was doing was making his wrists bleed. He slumped down on the ground again. They'd taken the Colt Python from him, of course, and searched him thoroughly. As yet, they hadn't tied him in with the little boat that had chugged past their stinkin' village earlier. He was sitting there, the night drifting toward dawn, and wondering why he hadn't just let Ariana do her bit and ignore the fact that she was lying to him. But if he had—he realized with a mirthless smile—they'd both be here together, now. Camacho's men, watching the grave, would have nabbed them both, and by now they'd have gotten the truth from Ariana or killed her. So maybe it was best this way, after all. He wanted to get back to her and choke her himself.

Time lost itself in the silent blackness of the little clay cubicle and Logan concluded that escape could only come through some break when he was taken outside. There was a small wooden door and he heard the sound of a guard on the other side of it. He sat there, still trying to piece together what Ariana had been after in Panico's mouth, and why. She still didn't fit into this kind of thing. But she was in it. Very much in it. Suddenly he heard the bolt of the door being pulled back. He got up and saw the door open. It was a woman, and he glimpsed the white, cotton scoop-necked blouse and skirt. He thought it was the woman who'd been with Camacho, until he heard the voice.

"There you are, you bastard," she said. She closed the door behind her and came toward him.

"I'll be damned," Logan said. "How the hell did you do it?"

"The guard? He was easy. I took these clothes from one of the women and just walked up to him. He thought I was one of the village belles coming over to be friendly. I got him to put down the gun and then I hit him with it."

"I was thinking about the piranhas," he admitted.

"Oh, that," she sniffed. "I got lucky. A big, fat piece of drift-wood came downriver and landed against the island. I just laid down on it and paddled to shore with my hands. Now, what did you do with Panico?"

"Nothing. Get these damned ropes off me," he said.

He saw her pull a knife from her belt and hold it in her hand, motionless. "Not until you tell me what you did with Panico," she said. "I saw the grave dug up and empty. Where did you hide the body?"

"Noplace," he repeated. "They nabbed me red-handed, or maybe it's dead-handed. Anyway, I was pulling him out when they came out of the woods. They must have decided to put him someplace else for a while."

She cut down on the wrist bonds with the knife and Logan felt his arms come free.

"Courtesy of the guard," she said, waving the knife.

"How did you know I was here?" Logan asked, rubbing his wrists.

"Your burlap sack was still by the grave. I thought, first, you'd had to make a quick exit with the body. Then I saw the guard standing in front of this place, the only one with a guard in front of it. I figured it had to hold either you or Panico. Or maybe both of you."

"Disappointed?" he asked, grimly. He felt her hand on his arm. There was contriteness in her voice.

"I told you I'd explain it all to you in time. You refused to wait," she said. "Please give me a chance to make you understand."

"Oh, you'll get a chance at that, you can count on it," he answered. "And it better be good. But first I'm getting your pal, Panico, and find out what he has to say. Let's see, now, it was the two lateral incisors, two anterior molars and one upper canine. How's that for a quick read?"

"Logan," she said, a catch in her voice. "Please don't interfere. Just let me do what I have to do and we can get out of here."

"Interfere? Come on, baby, you must be kidding. It's my way from here on in. Either that or I'm taking the first, last and only boat leaving this glamour spot tonight."

He waited as she hesitated. Even in the blackness he thought he could see the set of her jaw and her eyes, dark, reflecting the way her mind was clicking off the possibilities. She needed him. She couldn't lug the corpse back alone. Or, probably even find it on her own. There was no telling what she might run into, now. He gave her twenty seconds. She took fifteen.

"All right, we do it your way," she said. Logan grinned in the dark.

"Smart girl," he said. "Let's move."

He opened the door a crack and looked out into a semicircle of clay huts. The guard's body lay on the ground, alongside the rifle. Logan picked up the gun and smashed him on the temple again with the butt. "Insurance," he grunted. He gazed up at the sky. It told him that in less than an hour it would be dawn.

"I don't think they'd stash Panico in anyone's parlor," he said. "Let's try these huts."

They moved on silent feet to the nearest hut, opening the door carefully, only to find it empty. So was the next, and the next. They were only two from the end when they found the naked corpse lying on the ground inside the hut. Logan cast another look at the lightening sky.

"No time for any dentistry now," he said. "We take him with us. I wish to hell you'd brought my burlap sack."

Making a face, the tall, lean man scooped up the naked corpse. He slung it over one shoulder and started out with it. It wasn't heavy, just strangely slippery, as though it were made of a poor grade of plastic. When they reached the woods he dropped the corpse to the ground and, holding one arm, pulled it along after him.

"Can't you carry it?" Ariana asked. "It seems so, well, indecent this way, dragging it along like a piece of beef."

"Don't flatter him," Logan said. "You want to carry him?"

That ended the conversation and they were silent till they reached the raft at the edge of the river. Logan cast another anxious look at the sky. He knew all hell would break loose when dawn came and he wanted to be aboard the *Urchin*. "You hold and I'll paddle?" he said, but Ariana had the paddle in hand already. He shrugged and laid the corpse over his lap as he sat, yoga-fashion, in the raft. It was a tight fit.

"Get going," he said tersely. "This place is going to be alive with Camacho's boys within the hour."

"You think they'll suspect us of heading for the river?"

"I think they'll look everywhere. They'll cover all the bases. Besides, this row in the moonlight does nothing for me. Your friend here is a lousy conversationalist."

She paddled steadily and the sky grew lighter steadily. They reached the *Sea Urchin* just as the dawn came up in its first, misty-gray light. Carrying Panico under one arm, he pulled himself aboard the *Urchin*, tossed the corpse on the deck and took in the little raft as Ariana came up. He saw something metal glint in her hand as she knelt down beside the corpse. He turned to watch her and saw it was a dentist's pliers. She forced the jaws open on the corpse and Logan could see the grimace around her mouth, her lips drawn tight, and the strained tension of her face as she fought to control her feelings. He knelt down a few paces from her and watched as she extracted first one tooth, then another, then another, checking with the dental chart each time. Finally she was done and she had the five teeth clenched in her fist. She got up and Logan noticed the dry paleness of her face, her hard breathing.

"I'll take those," he said quietly.

"No," she said. "Please, Logan. Stay out of this. I have what I came for. Let's just go."

"Let's have them." His voice was colder, deeper.

"Why, Logan?" she asked, despair in her voice. "We can go now, so let's go. It's not your concern."

"Maybe it wasn't, once. It is now. The five choppers, Ariana. Give."

"They don't matter, now, Logan," she said. Her eyes were begging him, her voice imploring. "Let's just leave while we can."

"They do matter to me," he said. "What I'm doing matters. Why I'm doing it matters. Truth matters. Give, doll, or I'll knock yours out to go with the five you have."

He held out his hand. As she dropped the five teeth into it he saw her eyes turning from despair to anger. Logan took the teeth and went down into the cabin and pulled down the fold-out table. He knew that by now the village of Quechayo was erupting. He ought to get under way. But he also knew that once he did so it would take every bit of his concentration to get them back downriver alive. There could be no sandbars, no hang-ups, and there'd have to be speed. Once under way there'd not be another chance for him to get at the truth, not until they'd reached the wide-open waters of the Pacific and that was at best an even-money bet, now. So he had to take the time now to learn the truth. It wouldn't be there to take later, Camacho or no Camacho.

He laid the five teeth out on tire little table, took out his small fishing box and picked up a good, strong three-inch marlin hook. Working quickly, he dug at the filling in the center of the first tooth. He dug hard, casting a look at Ariana. She stood against the bunk, arms folded across her lovely breasts, glowering at him. The filling crumbled and came loose under the sharp point of the hook. He got the hook into a corner, pulled, and the whole thing came out and with it a tiny, rolled piece of material. He picked it up and smoothed it out. It was a tiny piece of microfilm.

"Interesting fillings your friend Panico has," he commented as he took a magnifying glass from the chart drawer. The message on the microfilm leaped in legibility under the magnifying glass and he read it aloud.

"Bechano: 776-654-ooG," he read, frowning. He laid the little piece of microfilm aside and dug the fishhook into the filling inside the next tooth, certain of what he'd find. The filling came out and with it a second piece of microfilm. Once more he read it aloud and this time a slow smile spread over his face as he did so.

"Alvarez: 45533-22G," he intoned and cast Ariana a glance.

"Logan, let's get away from here. Please," she said.

"One more," he said, picking up the third tooth, the molar. "This won't hurt a bit. Or will it?"

But the third one did hurt. He saw it in her black eyes as he read from the tiny bit of film that came out with the filling.

"dos Vayez: 881-00-343G," he read. He saw the pain deep inside her eyes as, his face stem, hard, he took the piece of microfilm and held it up to her.

"Your father?" he said and Ariana nodded.

"My brother, too," she added. Logan held up the last two of the teeth.

"In one of these?" he asked and she nodded. Her eyes blinked, slowly, carefully.

"These are microfilm records of numbered accounts in a Swiss bank, aren't they?" he said quietly. He didn't need an answer. Her silence was more then enough, her pain-filled eyes an exclamation point to it.

"What is your father in the Peruvian Government?"

"He is minister of Economic Development."

"Your brother?"

"Purchasing agent for the Defense Department." She anticipated his question. "Alvarez is head of internal security forces. The others are both cabinet ministers."

Logan dropped the two remaining teeth and the three tiny bits of microfilm into a small plastic bag he took out of the fishing box. He gazed at the girl as he did so. The pieces were all finally falling into place and, as he'd feared, they were falling into the wrong places for him, ugly places, sordid, corrupt places.

"Your father and brother, Alvarez, the others, they've been using their position to play in graft and corruption and stealing," he said. "And they've been putting a bundle away in numbered accounts in Swiss banks. Nice going."

Ariana was opening her mouth to say something, a denial, probably, but she ended up saying nothing.

"Where did old Panico fit in?" Logan asked.

"He was a cousin of Alvarez," she answered. "He took the monies to Switzerland for deposit. This way, if he were caught, there'd be nothing on him to implicate anyone, no instructions, no deposit slips, no account numbers, nothing."

"No wonder you wanted him back so badly," Logan mused aloud. "And who says the dead can't talk? And what about you, Ariana? Where do you come into this?"

"I never knew anything about it until a month ago, after Panico was killed, quite by accident, when the guerrillas attacked a government force he was with. My father told me everything then. I was the only one they could trust to try and get the teeth. All efforts to get at the body had failed."

"Blood being thicker than water and all that sort of thing," Logan added. "So you agreed to go right in with their little plan. That makes you no damn better than they are, just one more crook and lying thief."

He saw Ariana's eyes lose their hurt look and a fire flare in them. "Try something else, like human, or weak," she said. "I'll admit to that. I grew up in my world and I want to keep it. In my country, people's worlds are further apart than in yours. When I learned that my world, or some of it, anyway, had been bought by stolen money, I was shocked and hurt. I couldn't believe it. They convinced me how true it was. Being hurt and shocked and disillusioned is one thing. Loving your father and brother is something else. You don't turn your back on your family. You don't turn your back on all the things you've grown up to enjoy and want and believe in."

"Why not?" Logan heard the harshness of his voice. "Didn't you learn that corruption is corruption, that stealing is stealing, that wrong is wrong? Didn't they teach you that in all those fancy schools?"

"You can't understand at all, can you?" she asked, her eyes wide, sad, now.

"Sure I can. It happens all the time," he said. "It's more important to be comfortable than honest. But a crook is still a crook, no matter how comfortable he is."

"And who gave you the right to be so moral, to judge so?"

"I'm not being moral. I'm just mad at being sold a bill of goods. I don't like being swindled on anything. You said you were the good guys, against the Commie revolutionaries trying to wreck your country. Hell, all you're after is protecting your own racket. Maybe Camacho ought to have these choppers. Maybe they're the good guys."

"They're swine," Ariana blazed. "They'd use that evidence to bring down the government. They'd use it to take over and turn the country into a dictatorship run by Camacho."

He half-smiled to himself. In her own, crazy way she was terribly upset at that thought. The idea of her father and brother stealing the government blind, of five highly placed officials being part of a corrupt regime, didn't phase her. That wasn't all that unusual, he concluded. We're never as bothered by our own misdeeds as we are by those of others. And corruption was a built-in part of the political scene. It became almost acceptable. Revolutionary movements were an outside threat. Hell, he reminded himself, he didn't know Camacho or what he stood for anymore than he really knew the make-up of the Peruvian Government. He wasn't going to make political decisions. There was an established government and there was Camacho and they could fight their differences out with each other. He kept remembering a certain character once called an idealist on a little island called Cuba. Maybe Camacho was another Castro. Maybe he was something better. All maybes. The only real thing he had was evidence of five corrupt thieves and he knew that he would act on that. He wasn't sure yet just how, but he knew he would find a way. He put the little plastic packet into his pocket.

Ariana's eyes met his and he felt sorry for this beautiful and headstrong girl. She'd been torn by this. He was even sorrier she hadn't come up with a better answer to it.

"What now, Logan?" he heard her ask, quietly. "Now that you know everything, what are you going to do?"

A rifle shot supplied his answer.

"Get the hell out of here, first," he said, racing up to the deck. He stayed low, crouching, as he made the pilot house. There were three of Camacho's men on the shore and as he looked over at them he saw two disappear into the woods. Ariana had followed him on deck.

"Stay low and get the anchor up," he said, kicking the engine over. The Diesel coughed, then roared into life. The man on shore sent another shot at the boat and he heard the slug whistle past the pilot house. Ariana had crawled into the pilot house now and stood beside him. The *Sea Urchin* started moving forward and Logan steered around the far side of the island, away from the shore where Camacho's men waited. It was the wrong side of the island to take but the Tinina was hardly crowded with river traffic.

"Here, take this key and open that locker," Logan said to the girl. He watched as she pulled open the gun locker and gave him back the key. She took out one of the rifles, the Mossberg 640-K with the telescopic sight.

"You get behind the rail and shoot at anything that heads for us or shoots at us," he said. "I'm going to keep us moving. If they really try to rush us I'll join you. Other than that, I want to stay at the wheel. There's extra ammo on the floor of the closet."

"All right," she said. "But first, I want that little package back."

Logan looked around to see the Mossberg aimed at his chest, Ariana's face behind it calm, immobile.

"Go to hell," he said and turned away. He'd call her bluff. Without him, she wouldn't get more than a few miles downriver. The Mossberg's roar was deafening inside the pilot house and Logan felt the bullet crease his belly as it tore by him and imbedded itself into the wood. He jumped back from the wheel in reflex action.

"You're crazy," he said. "How far do you think you'd get without me?"

"I don't know," she said, her voice tight. "Just give me the package. Now."

He had thought to reason with her, or that she'd see for herself she needed him but he realized that she wasn't reasoning any longer. She was reacting only to what she'd done, the pressures that had been on her, to the things he'd said that had struck deep. It was in the wild-frightened look of her eyes, all of it, the inner turmoil, the panic, the emotional torture. Just then, the *Urchin's* nose came around the end of the island and three shots rang out. Logan dropped down, automatically, and he saw Ariana do the same. Staying low, he moved across the floor of the pilot house almost to her side. But the Mossberg was still pointed at him.

"Let's do our fighting later or neither of us will get back," he said and suddenly she was against him, trembling in his arms, her face buried in his shoulder.

"Logan, I don't want to fight with you," she said. "I want you to come with me. Please."

"We'll see," he said, letting a smile cross his face. Her deep eyes were searching his, now, looking for some sign of reassurance and compassion. He put a hand against her cheek, tenderly.

"We'll talk more, later," he said. "We'll find time. Right now you better get down to that rail."

She nodded, her eyes suddenly misty, and crawled away, moving outside to the rail of the *Urchin*. He could see her from the pilot-house window as he took the wheel. The shots had come from the shore and he saw the same figure ducking back into the trees as the boat swung out into midriver. Logan increased speed as another shot rang out, passing harmlessly over the top of the pilot house. A few more shots whistled past them as they moved downriver and he saw Ariana looking up at him.

"What are they doing?" she called.

"Keeping pace with us," he said. "They probably have two or three men moving along with us just at the line of the trees. They're making sure we don't ditch the boat and take off."

"And the others?"

"Preparing a surprise for us, I'm sure." He slowed the engines as he saw the water curling up on the surface, indicating a sandbar beneath. He moved the *Urchin* across it carefully, feeling the churning of her propellers in the shallowness of the water. Then he gunned her again and they moved forward. But he knew, grimly, that real speed was impossible. On shore, even moving through the jungle trails, Camacho and his men could make better time. And they were there, someplace behind the green wall. He stepped to the gun closet and took out two more of the rifles. He put one beside the wheel and handed the other out the window to Ariana.

"Stay low," he cautioned as she moved over to take it. "Keep it with you just in case they try a sudden rush. It'll save time reloading."

She had returned to the rail and sat on the deck, looking up at him at the wheel.

"Logan," she called to him. "I would have told you everything. Later. I would have. Please believe me."

"I believe you," he said, and he wasn't lying. She would have told him the truth, he knew. After she'd shown him all the things of her world, after she felt she'd softened him up enough so he could no longer reject what she offered. It wouldn't have worked. He knew that and he knew that was something she couldn't make herself believe. She'd lived all her young life in a world where having what you wanted was taken for granted, where pleasure was the most important thing in it. In that kind of world, all the principles and the teachings are nothing more than pleasant abstractions.

"Logan," he heard her call again and he peered out the window at her. "What about him?" She was pointing a finger at the corpse on the other side of the deck. He'd forgotten about Panico in their hurry to move on and the hot sun was beginning to make him something less then fragrant. He locked the wheel in place and scurried down to the deck.

"Let's make a show of it," he said. "It'll keep them busy a while."

He dragged the corpse to the side facing Camacho's men and heaved it into the river, watching for a moment as the current immediately seized it and started to push it toward shore. He knew he wasn't the only one watching and he smiled, grimly, as he went back to the wheel. Another dammed island was coming up and he began to steer around it. He would be on the far side when the body hit shore but he knew there'd be a scramble of arms waiting to pull it in. He turned his attention back to making the best time they could. Camacho had apparently faded away with his main force. Logan knew better. He had one girl, six rifles, a boat and a lousy little river between himself and Camacho. He felt the little plastic package in his pocket. Maybe bargaining would be a lot smarter than fighting. Their fives against the microfilm and the two teeth. Maybe Camacho ought to have it, anyway. But Logan tossed away the thought as quickly as it had entered his mind. That would be taking sides and he had no right to do that. He looked down at Ariana on the deck, at the long-stemmed beauty of her and he doubted whether she'd let him even bargain with the guerrilla leader. Perhaps her idea of principles was vague and undefined but her loyalties were firm and clear. What the hell, he wasn't much for bargaining, anyway. Not unless there was no other way, and that remained to be seen.

CHAPTER NINE

I t was late afternoon and they'd only had an occasional stray shot from the shore. Ariana felt the tension inside her building up to almost unbearable heights. Only the presence of the tall, lean, hard-faced man at the wheel kept her from diving overboard and fleeing, running from all of it, from her decisions, her loyalties, her desires. Why did they always have to conflict so? She glanced up at Logan, at the hard handsomeness of his face and she wanted so to be in his arms again, and to feel his hands caressing her body. It was all right, then, when he made love to her. Everything wrong disappeared. It would be night, soon. Maybe she could have that world once more. She shook her head angrily. The night wouldn't bring safety. It would only bring increased danger. His eyes would not be for her but for the dark shadows of the shore. His arms would hold the cold steel of a rifle and not the soft warmth of her breasts. Dammit, she swore, silently. Somehow, she had to find a way to reach this uncompromising man. She couldn't lose him. She needed the strength he had to give, the courage that could make her do what was right, not what was best. If she could wrap herself around his magnificent body once more, perhaps he'd realize he could not turn away from her. She suddenly laughed, silently. She'd often talked of love, with the girls in college, her friends, the usual social chatter of and around the subject. But she'd never come up with a definition that really satisfied her and now, here on this horrible little river, with her life in danger, she'd come up with as good a one as any she'd ever heard. Love is someone you can't turn away from, no matter what. She looked up at Logan, his deep, probing eyes shifting from side to side, and she knew he could always turn away. Yet, he must have loved once, terribly deeply. No matter, she could bring enough for two and in time, he'd love again as he had once.

It was getting dark and they were rounding a bend in the river. She moved from the rail and went up to the pilot house, just in time to see Logan cut the engines.

"Look at what they've rigged up for us," he commented and she gazed ahead to see the double row of rowboats and canoes stretched across the river from shore to shore. Six guerrillas with rifles were spaced across the double row of boats. Each boat had a burlap sack or blanket stretched across it and Logan brought the *Urchin* to a halt. It was nearly dark and he dropped a small hand anchor in midriver, just heavy enough to hold them still.

"Why are you stopping?" Ariana asked. "If you got up speed, we could crash right through those little boats."

"It would seem so," Logan said. Ariana searched his eyes.

"What are you thinking?" she asked.

"That Camacho isn't stupid," he answered. "That would occur to him, too."

"But he put them there?"

"He probably figures we'll wait till dark and then slam through. I think his little boats are some sort of booby trap and I'm going to find out."

"Meanwhile?"

"Meanwhile we sit tight till it's dark."

"And while we're sitting here they can swim out to board us."

"No, not now, anyway. They've set up this one and they'll go with it. They'll wait for us to make the next move."

He felt the girl's head against his shoulder as he moved back against the wall. He slid down to the floor to rest and she came with him, her body pressed against his. He turned to her and found her lips as the blackness closed over them and her tongue was eager as ever, searching, probing, asking. She took his hand and thrust it against her breast and gasped as he let his thumb gently caress her pink tip. Finally, he pulled back.

"Easy, honey," he murmured. "This is not the time."

"I know," she said. "I just wanted you for a moment, anyway. I needed that. We will talk again, when this is over, you promised."

"I promised," he said, getting to his feet and pulling her with him. "Think we're downriver enough to be out of piranha waters?" he asked.

"Oh, yes," she said, quickly. Logan pointed to a switch on the instrument panel.

"This puts on the searchlight. You can make it revolve and direct it from these two little levers alongside. Give me two minutes and then put on the light. Keep it pointed down into the water and revolving around the boat. That way you can catch anyone trying a sneak approach. When I come back, I'll swim under the boat and rap three times against the port side. Turn off the light, then."

"Where are you going?"

"To have a look at those boats," he said, starting down to the deck. He moved over the rail and lowered himself quietly into the water. It was warm and thick. He swam downriver with slow, measured strokes, noiselessly. As he neared the line of rowboats that had been stretched across the river he saw the outlines of the two nearest men sitting on the boats. He dived and swam underwater, passing under the double-row of boats and surfacing on the other side. Treading water, he moved to the two rowboats in between the first and second sentry. Grasping the gunwale lightly, he hung there for a moment, watching the sentries, ready to submerge in an instant But the two men peered steadily ahead toward the *Urchin* a half-mile up river. Slowly, he reached one arm up and pulled back the blanket inside the boat. There were two clusters of dynamite sticks, one at each end of the boat, with the fuse string running across into the next boat. He put back the cover and slipped below the surface of the water again, swimming back beneath the boats, staying underwater till he was a safe distance from them before surfacing. He hadn't looked into the other boats. There was no need to do so. He knew they'd have the same cargo, more dynamite. He saw the *Urchin's* searchlight revolving around her and he swam toward it, surface diving when he neared the swiftly moving circle of light. He came up under the port side and rapped three times against the hull. The light went out and he surfaced, drawing a deep breath. He took the line Ariana tossed out and climbed aboard to rest on the deck, catching his breath.

"Dynamite inside the boats," he said. "As soon as we began a run to smash through, one of those six jokers they put there as fake sentries would light the fuse and they'd all take off. It'd blow up in our faces as we reached the boats."

Ariana's face was set, frightened. "So what do we do now?" she questioned.

"Beat them at their own game," he said. "That's why I came back. I want my cigarette lighter in the drawer beneath the wheel. You'll find a fish-bait knife there, too." She was back in moments with both things.

"Give me another five minutes then switch the light back on and keep it revolving," Logan said. "It'll keep them thinking we're both on board."

He kissed her, taking her by surprise, and grinned at her. "That's for luck," he said and disappeared over the side. Once

again in the tepid water, he swam silently, using long, deliberate strokes, grateful for the inky blackness of the night. Nearing
the line of rowboats and canoes, he surface dived again to come
out behind them. He stayed near the end of the line of boats
and came up behind the first of the six waiting guerrillas. This
would be tricky, he knew. One wrong move, one sound on the
man's part, and the whole idea would go up in smoke. But he
had to be fast and being fast would cause problems of its own. If
the man toppled into the water, one of the others would hear it,
peer over and find him gone. He was almost directly behind the
guerrilla, now, and he drew the razor-sharp bait knife from his
belt. The man was sitting crosslegged in the boat. Logan, moving
noiselessly, rested his left hand lightly on the gunwale of the boat
and then, with one motion, pulled himself half-out of the water
and brought the knife around in a fast, vicious slash. It almost
severed the man's head and at the same instant, Logan had his
other arm around the guerrilla's body and was pulling him from
the boat and into the water, lowering him silently into the river.
He submerged with the man, keeping him underwater just to be
sure. Finally, he let the limp body go and pushed it away, letting
the river current carry it downstream. Holding onto the boat,
he reached in and severed the fuse on both clusters of dynamite
sticks. He hung there a moment, pausing for breath, drying his
hands by rubbing them along the inside of the rowboat. Then
he took the fuse, tied it together and bypassed the dynamite in
the first boat. He made his way to the second and cut those fuses
also. Then he spliced the cut fuse onto the other and bypassed the
dynamite on the second boat. He now had a long fuse running to
the dynamite in the third boat where the second sentry sat.

Once more he submerged to come up again directly behind
the man. He was about to draw the knife from his belt when
something made the man turn, perhaps instinct. He saw Logan,

half-out of the water, and his eyes widened. There was only time to clasp a hand over the man's mouth and pull. The sentry came off the boat and into the water with Logan's hand still over his mouth. Logan submerged and felt the man's hands clawing at his eyes. He released his hold on the man's mouth and grabbed him by the throat. He held tightly as the man thrashed and kicked and swallowed more of the river. With the desperate strength of the dying, he twisted and tore free of Logan's grip. He started for the surface but Logan got his ankle and pulled hard. The man came down and suddenly Logan felt his struggles turn off, almost the way a wind-up toy turns off with a sudden cessation, a last, feeble shudder. Logan's lungs were searing. He hadn't had time to take a proper breath before diving and he struck out for the surface, seeing blackness before his eyes, his head starting to pound dangerously. He broke the surface and gasped in the life-giving air and saw he'd drifted down some twenty yards from the boats. He trod water for a few minutes to regain his breath and then returned to the third boat. Once again he cut the fuses to the two dynamite clusters and spliced the cut pieces onto the long fuse that now ran across three boats to the fourth one. Enough, he decided.

He swam, underwater, back to the first of the rowboats and surfaced again. Taking out the cigarette lighter, he lit the fuse and waited to make certain it had caught properly. Then he dived beneath the boats and struck out for the *Urchin*. The long fuse would give him time to reach the *Urchin* before it burned down to the dynamite in the fourth boat. This time he paid no attention to the revolving fight and called out to Ariana as he swam into it. He saw her put down the Mossberg and douse the beam. He clambered aboard, rested for a moment on one knee, and then hurried to the wheelhouse. He turned the engines on to full and the *Urchin* roared into life. There was no time to pull the hand anchor. As the boat roared forward, her prow sending up sprays of the murky river water, the night suddenly exploded in a gigantic fireworks display as the dynamite went up. Against the red-orange flames he saw bits and pieces of rowboat and canoe sail into the air, silhouetted against the brilliance of the flash. In seconds, a barrage of rifle fire erupted from both shores, most of it wild, whistling harmlessly around the *Urchin* as she sped through the water. He kept the throttle wide open and the brilliant night-lighting flash of the explosion disappeared as the *Urchin* hit the debris of the rowboats and sailed on through.

"Put on the light," Logan shouted at the girt "I can't see where the hell I'm going!"

The searchlight came on, sending its blue-white eye ahead, lighting a path for them, and the rifle fire came to a halt. Ariana's arms were around his neck, her soft breasts pressing into his back as she came up behind him.

"We've made it," she exclaimed happily.

"They'll try again."

He felt his eyes growing heavy-lidded, and fatigue was wrapping itself around him like a too-tight suit. He held on till they skirted another of the islands and then he pulled into midriver and dropped the regular anchor.

"I've got to get some sleep," he said. "Or I won't be worth a damn come morning. You too."

Ariana nodded. "We'll take turns standing watch," Logan said. "Two-hour shifts. I have a feeling they'll let us alone for tonight."

He lay down on the floor of the pilot house and in seconds he was asleep. Ariana sat on the seat by the ship's wheel, the Mossberg in her hands. Despite what the lean man had said, she felt confident. About a lot of things.

CHAPTER TEN

Logan took over in two hours and watched the girl's sleeping form on the floor beside him, the regular rise and fall of her breasts, the soft, long curve of her thighs and, despite his fatigue, he felt himself wanting to move down on top of her. She was a strange girl, this Ariana dos Vayez, so maturely determined in some things, so much of a little girl in others. And she got to you. With her beauty she got to you. With her wild, passionate body she got to you. Yes, even with her wrong-headed loyalties, she got to you. But he knew that if they got down the Tinina, if they got away from the infuriated guerrilla leader, they'd still part bitterly. He wouldn't walk her side of the street and she still hoped he would. He knew that. He could see it in her eyes, that and something more. He'd seen it in the eyes of many women. They had learned that he couldn't give all that they wanted. Some he had told beforehand, and they didn't believe him. Others he only told after, and they didn't believe him. But they all came to accept it, some with anger, some with bitterness, some with sadness. Yes, there'd been a few who managed some form of understanding, but only a few. He wondered how it would be with Ariana. Furious anger, he told himself. Her passion and her temper would see to that. And so he contented himself with watching her lovely body stir in its sleep and remembering the warm feel of her legs around him, her lips on his. She woke some three hours later and he caught a few more hours, finally waking refreshed enough to go on. The sun was out in full and Ariana made coffee.

"See anything during the night?" he asked.

"Nothing," she said. "Not a sign. Do you think they've given up?"

His eyes answered her. "Didn't you say Camacho's people control most of this area down to the coast?" he asked.

"Yes," she said. "But we made good time yesterday. We could reach the coast by midnight, couldn't we?"

"If we can keep going steadily," he answered. "But they've gone ahead of us again, you can bet on it. They've got to. It's their only way to get at us, to set up something and wait."

He pulled up anchor and started the *Urchin* downriver, faster than he should, his eyes once again glued to the water ahead, watching for current changes, churning whirlpools, all the signs of shallow bottom. But they made good time and he was beginning to think that perhaps he'd been overly pessimistic. Maybe Camacho had retired after the *Urchin* had got through his elaborate booby trap. Yet it was not like the man. He had seen too much pride in those eyes and the guerrilla knew that whatever it was Panico had that made him valuable was now in their possession. No, he wouldn't quit till they reached the Pacific. The afternoon sun came, paused high in the heavens and started to slip down toward evening, and still there was no sign of the guerrilla force. It was too quiet, and as they nosed around one of the sharper bends, his fears were confirmed. Camacho he saw, had gathered every one of his crummy little group. Across the river, stretched from tree to tree, they had put a rope bridge. It would just clear the *Urchin's* pilot-house roof, and it was sagging with the weight of the guerrillas clinging to it. He slowed the boat and surveyed the scene. Beyond the bridge—in rowboats, canoes, dugouts and rafts—the rest of his men waited on both sides. He slowed the *Urchin* further, barely moving forward, as his mind raced. He couldn't see the guerrilla leader who had probably stayed on shore. His guess was confirmed as he heard Camacho's voice, amplified by a megaphone.

"You out there," he heard the man's voice. "You, Logan. Listen to me." The guerrilla paused for a moment and then went on. "Give us what you took from Panico and we will let you go," he called. "We saw from his body that you took five teeth from him. We want what was in those teeth."

He lapsed into silence and waited for a reply. He didn't get one. Logan was too busy trying to figure out their best chance to get through and he decided there was no best chance. The forward mast would hit the rope bridge. It would probably snap off, but whether it did or didn't, it'd knock a few of them off into the water. The rest figured to drop down aboard the boat as it passed under them. Then the others in their little craft would swarm in from both sides to board them. Logan looked at Ariana. There was fear in her eyes and angry determination in the set of her jaw. He asked himself why the hell he didn't just give Camacho what he wanted and he knew the answer at once. Stubbornness.

Logan reached into the gun closet and took out another of the rifles, leaning it against the wood near the wheel.

"You stay in here," he told the girl. "It's as good a spot as any. Get up against the side and just keep shooting."

He glanced at her again. "Want to change your mind and give up?" he asked. Her head shook impatiently. "I'll be right back," he said. He jumped down to the deck, moving quickly, and down into the large hatchway to the engines. He took only a few moments and when he returned to the pilot house he no longer had the little plastic package with him. He took the wheel, reversed engines to gain more headway, and pulled the throttle to full speed ahead. He pointed the *Urchin* for the right-hand end of the rope bridge as she sent river water spraying up from her prow. Just beyond the bridge, where the boats were gathered on either side, the river was just wide enough for a tight circle. If he timed it right, and had a little luck, he'd make the boarding party work for their dinner.

The *Urchin's* mast slammed into the rope bridge, bent, and snapped. But guerrillas were dropping into the river on all sides as they passed under the bridge. He saw three of them come down on the forward deck. Ariana's Mossberg was firing and they never got a chance to get up. He heard the thump of two more landing, one on the starboard deck amidship, the other aft. Ariana poked the rifle out the right window and fired. He heard the man topple overboard. They'd passed the rope bridge, now, and he swung the wheel hard to port and locked it in place. The *Urchin,* moving at full speed, started to wheel in a tight circle, slamming into rowboats and canoes, scattering them in all directions. The circling vessel made boarding much harder and almost eliminated any attempts from the port side inside the circle. The door of the pilot house flew open but Logan had been expecting it and his rifle barked first. The guerrilla arched backward and fell to the deck.

"He was from the bridge," Logan commented. "You cover the port side. I'll take the starboard."

He ran on deck, a rifle in each hand. Three of them had managed to get a hold forward and were climbing up the side. He fired three times and they were gone. A bullet slammed into the wood a half-inch from his head. He dived flat on to the deck, whirled and fired at the figure climbing over the stern rail. The guerrilla fell heavily, landing in a crumpled heap on the deck. He heard Ariana's rifle firing on the port side and then he saw more clambering up over the stern. He moved aft, firing as he went, and more figures toppled back into the river. Then he heard the thump of boats against the bow, whirled and saw another cluster of figures climbing over the rail. He fired and the rifle barked once and fell silent. He threw it at a black-haired figure climbing aboard amidship and saw it smash into his temple. He slid back into the river. Logan ran forward, firing with the other rifle. Two figures fell to lie across the rail, half-in and half-out of the boat. A shot grazed his head and he felt the trickle of wet across his scalp. He dropped to one knee and whirled, firing at the figure on the aft deck. The guerrilla dived to safety behind the pilot house. They were coming over the starboard rail now, leaping up and hanging on, and though he was firing as fast as he could, there was always another one clambering aboard. More shots were coming his way and he dropped to the deck and started to crawl toward the pilot house. He heard Ariana scream, and the sound of glass shattering. He got to his feet, firing furiously, racing up the few steps to the pilot house. His rifle went dead just as he reached the pilot-house door. Ariana was gone, and he saw the broken glass window at the port side where she'd been dragged through. Then he heard Camacho's voice through the megaphone.

"*¡Parer!*" he called to his men and the firing stopped. Logan shut off the *Urchin's* engines and the vessel slowed at once. He stood by the instrument board, one hand on a switch lever.

"We have the girl, Logan," Camacho called. "Look out your left window. There is a gun at her temple."

Logan edged forward just enough to see the port deck. One of the guerrillas had his arm around Ariana's neck, his other hand holding a revolver against her temple.

"Now do we get what we want?" Camacho called out. Obviously, the man was watching through binoculars from the shore. Logan had a bull horn along the top edge of the pilot house and he turned it on.

"Camacho," he called, "I have my finger on a switch. If I press it what you want will disappear out of the bilge pump and into the river. It will never be seen again. Harm the girl and I'll press it."

There was silence. "All I have to do is press my finger and the information I have, all the evidence, is gone," Logan repeated. There was a long moment of silence and then Camacho replied.

"You would risk the girl for this evidence?" he asked.

"No," Logan said. "I just tell you if she is harmed, I press this switch."

"Then it appears we have a stalemate, *amigo,* no? And I don't like stalemates."

"I have a proposition," Logan called. "But I want the girl up here where I can see her, first."

Another moment of silence and then Camacho spoke to his man. "Take the girl to the pilot-house door where he can see her," he ordered. "But don't let go of her."

Logan waited and the smell of gunpowder, acrid and heavy, hung in the thick, humid air. Hand on the bilge pump switch, he watched as the guerrilla brought Ariana to the pilot-house doorway and stepped inside with her. He held the revolver to her temple.

"Now you see the girl, Logan," Camacho called. "What is your proposition? What are you getting out of this? Money?"

"Not that much," Logan answered. "The evidence I have will be put in the hands of the proper authorities. I promise you that. Alvarez and his group of thieves will be ousted from their posts in the government and punished."

'We will do the same thing if you give it to us."

"No. You will use it to further your revolution and I don't know if your revolution will be a good thing or not for the people of Peru. I don't know if you will be a friend or an enemy of democracy. I won't take sides."

"And if I don't believe you?" Camacho queried. Logan's lips tightened. The guerrilla leader had most of his people here, looking on, and certainly many of the uncommitted natives.

"Then we will both lose," Logan said. "This is your chance to show if you are really interested in the people, in a good government, or only in the glory of Camacho. Let me go and Alvarez and his group will be in jail in forty-eight hours. Camacho will have helped rid the people of Peru of five thieves. Force me to press this switch and there will be no evidence to prevent Alvarez and the others from continuing."

What happened next, Logan blamed himself for later. If he hadn't spelled it out so plainly maybe she wouldn't have acted. Ariana twisted, suddenly, and leaped across the pilot house, hands outstretched for the pump switch. The guerrilla fired and Logan saw her body shudder, twist and fall to the floor. She landed at his feet and the guerrilla stepped back, out of the wheelhouse, fear in his eyes. Logan was cradling the beautiful head in his arms and the black hair fell in cascades onto his chest.

"You little fool," he muttered and watched the red stain spreading, seeping. She opened her eyes and her hand made little motions. He lifted it and held it against his broad chest, and she smiled.

"You wouldn't have come with me, would you?" she asked.

"No," he said. She didn't deserve being lied to. "But I would have thought about it."

"It's better this way, then."

"No it isn't, dammit," he said. "Why did you have to play heroine?"

"I couldn't have done anything else. The past owns the future, or didn't I tell you that?"

His hand was stroking her cheek and he was shaking his head in disagreement when she half-rose, fighting down the pain, and he held her to him.

"Don't leave me here, Logan," she said. "Take me with you. Take me to where we first made love."

"I will," he said, quietly, and suddenly she was slumped in his arms and he stroked her hair for the last time. He got up and he heard Camacho's voice through the megaphone.

"I am sorry about the girl," the guerrilla leader said. "Was she your woman?"

"No," Logan answered slowly. "She was just someone I liked."

"You will do what you promised?" Camacho asked. "You will see that Alvarez and the others are jailed?"

"You can be goddamn sure of it," Logan said, cold fury in his voice. His eyes were not on the shore but on the lovely girl at his feet. "You can be goddammed sure."

"All right, I believe you," the guerrilla leader said. "Only a man who means what he says would be so determined."

Camacho gave crisp orders to his men and they dropped from the *Urchin* like so many flies. Logan started the engines, turned the nose of the boat downriver and moved forward. He saw the river widening and he knew that the blue waters of the Pacific were not far away. His eyes stared ahead, deep, and only those who knew him very well would have been able to see the pain inside them. He didn't want to think about the girl who lay at his feet but that was impossible. The past owns the future, she had said and he wondered whether she really believed that. Maybe for her it did. Maybe it did for a lot of people. But he couldn't help thinking that if he'd lied to her, if he'd made her believe he would go into her world with her, she would not have leaped for the pump switch. And so it was not the past that owned the future, that governed her action, but fear of having to live in a shadowed world. She'd been told she had to fight for that world, when she didn't have to fight for it at all. In a very real way, she had been used, sold a bill of goods just the way they'd sold him a bill of goods. Their lies to him were merely about the real purpose of a job. They'd lied to her about the real purpose of her life.

And so now she lay dead and there was the real crime. They would pay only for stealing monies, not for stealing a life. Logan glanced down at the girl. One of them would pay the full price. He'd see to that. The steel-cold hardness crept over him and he knew exactly what to do.

It was dark when he steered the boat into the waters of the Pacific and at once the cool winds swirled about him in a kind of welcome. He sailed back along the route they had taken and, at a certain spot, he stopped the boat. Reaching down, he picked up the girl, carefully, tenderly, and carried her down to the deck. He'd known prayers as a boy but they'd long been pushed back into the dim recesses of his mind. He remembered only something about the Lord giving and the Lord taking away.

When he returned to the pilot house he was alone.

CHAPTER ELEVEN

It was late afternoon when he sailed into the little cove in Panama. He found a spot and tied up at the wharf. He took the number Alvarez had given him from the chart drawer and went to the phone booth at the end of the quay. The man's voice almost leaped in excitement as Logan identified himself.

"I have a package for you," Logan said flatly. "I'll come right over with it. What is the address?"

Alvarez gave him a number on Campanile Street and Logan hailed a taxi. The house turned out to be large, stucco, and Alvarez was waiting at the door.

"Where's Ariana?" the man asked as he admitted Logan, his smooth urbanity unable to cloak his excitement.

"She couldn't come," Logan answered. He took the plastic package from his pocket and held it up for Alvarez to see. He wanted to make sure the man saw he had it, to bait him into the wrong move.

"This is going to be turned over to the President of your country," Logan said. "If I were you I'd resign now."

He saw the man's face darken and Alvarez was out of his chair. "What are you talking about?" he growled. His smooth, urbane exterior was disappearing fast.

"Your little racket," Logan said. "It's over, done with. I'm going to expose you, all of you."

Alvarez fought with himself a moment and managed one of his charming, controlled smiles.

"I understand," he said. "And perhaps I should have expected it. You want more money. All right, how much more?"

Logan's temper was nearing the boiling point. He didn't want conversation. He wanted action.

"Nothing, you bastard," he said. "I want you, behind bars, or dead. I'd like that even better."

He saw Alvarez's jaw tighten and the man's eyes bored into his.

"Give me that package," the man said. Logan started for the door. "Go screw yourself," he said. Out of the corner of his eye he saw Alvarez dart toward a desk in the corner of the room. A thin smile crossed the tall, mean man's face. This was it, what Logan wanted. He whirled and reached the desk at the same time that Alvarez yanked open the drawer and brought out a snub-barreled revolver. Logan's hand closed around Alvarez's wrist and he used his weight to slam the man's body back across the desk. He heard the revolver drop to the floor as Alvarez's arm bent backward. Logan was smiling, a cold, mirthless smile, as he smashed his fist into the man's jaw and watched him skid across the desk and into the wall.

"Now, you bastard," Logan said. "I'm going to save your country the expense of a trial."

He reached for the man but Alvarez, with the instinctive knowledge of every animal facing death, erupted in desperate strength. He kicked out and Logan managed to half-turn aside and take the blow on his arm. But it sent him skittering back a few feet. Alvarez leaped, landing atop him, his hands finding Logan's throat. Logan hit the man in the belly with all his strength. The hands left his throat and Alvarez doubled over in pain. A looping right sent the man somersaulting backward across the room and Logan felt the crack of his jawbone as the blow landed. Only the desperation of the cornered animal kept

Alvarez fighting. He lunged across the floor for the revolver lying beside the desk. Logan's foot reached it first and kicked it away. Then he reached down and hit the man again. Alvarez landed half-across the desk. But his hand closed around a steel letter opener, as sharply pointed as any knife. He rolled from the end of the desk and landed on his feet. As the big man came at him again, he lunged. Logan shifted his body a fraction and the letter opener tore through the folds of his shirt. He sent a short, hard right into Alvarez's stomach and the man tottered backward. But the weapon was still in his hand and he swung again with it as Logan moved in. Logan stepped back and avoided the blow, and his right flashed out like a bullwhip being snapped. It landed on Alvarez's shattered jaw and spun the man into the wall. He heard Alvarez's gasp of pain.

"That's for that beating I took in that stinkin' jail," Logan hissed. Alvarez collapsed against the wall, crumpling to the floor. Somehow, he still held onto the letter opener. Logan lifted him to his feet with one hand and rammed his fist into his face. Alvarez arched backward, half-turned in the air, and fell to the floor.

"That one was for Ariana," Logan said bitterly. He went over to the still, crumpled form and turned it over. The letter opener was deep into the man's abdomen. His hand still held the handle.

Logan straightened up and walked to the desk. He picked up the telephone and dialed long distance, Washington, D.C. He asked for Ted Russell, State Department, and went through a succession of secretaries. Finally the phone was picked up and a voice from the not-too-dim past spoke in his ear.

"I don't believe it," the voice said. "Say something so I know it's you."

"It's me, Ted," Logan answered. "I have something for you. You'll know what to do with it and how."

Logan spoke quickly, leaving out only a few details, and the two men exchanged brief comments with the quiet respect of friends. When he'd finished, Logan drew a deep breath and waited.

"Christ, what a story," Russell commented. "It'll sure help us with the top level of the Peruvian Government. Can you get the evidence and a statement to our Consul there?"

"I can be there in an hour."

"Great. I'll call him and they'll be ready and waiting for you. We'll take it from there. You say you've got names, account numbers, everything, eh?"

"Everything."

"Five of them, eh?"

"Five. But one's dead. Alvarez."

"You wouldn't like to tell me how he got dead, I suppose."

"You suppose right," Logan said flatly. He heard Russell chuckle, and then the man's voice grew serious again.

"Everything all right with you and the *Urchin*?" Russell asked gently.

"Fine," Logan said. "No help needed."

"Good. Anyway, you know what to do if there ever is." The man's voice paused for a moment and then went on. "Logan," he said. "Thanks. Take care of yourself."

"I will," the tall, lean man answered quietly. He put down the phone and thought of how a few words could say a lot. He stepped over the crumpled form on the floor and walked out of the house into the gathering dusk. He moved quickly, anxious to finish with this business.

It was night when a tubby little vessel sailed out of Panama Harbor. She wasn't going anywhere in particular, just out into the night and the sea, where the world couldn't crowd in on you so.

www.ingramcontent.com/pod-product-compliance
Lightning Source LLC
Chambersburg PA
CBHW030133260626
47156CB00008B/2929